Niiva used to be a farmer's daughter with every stereotype that went along with it. Her hormones raged out of control, and her body usually followed.

Now, she is on Imrahl, one of thousands of humans abducted to work with the Rrassic in their war efforts, and she has been kept away from the eligible warriors in a bid to keep her doing what she does best, farming.

One night after working late on a shipment, she finds herself facing a drunk human and a few of the leonine Regiz-Rrassic. They mistake her for a male and begin to get aggressive when another of their kind steps in to break it up. Argo takes notice of her, and it spells the end of her life as a harvester and a fast track into the Breeder compound.

Resistance is no longer a priority.

Resisting Desire
Copyright © 2019 Viola Grace
ISBN: 978-1-4874-2469-5
Cover art by Angela Waters

Published by eXtasy Books Inc or
Devine Destinies, an imprint of eXtasy Books Inc

Look for us online at:
www.eXtasybooks.com or www.devinedestinies.com

Resisting Desire
Brace for Humanity Book 4

By

Viola Grace

OTHER BOOKS IN THIS SERIES

Untrained Fascination
Heart of the Hunted
Overseer's Chain

Chapter One

The labourers gathered around the announcement board, and Niiva stood behind them.

Rita giggled. "They want us to audition to become peacekeepers."

Niiva blinked. "What?"

"Peacekeepers. To represent humanity on Imrahl. They want them to take Hunter training, and those that pass will gain a position on one of the teams." Rita read the information as it scrolled on the screen.

Niiva turned away. "That is fascinating. I am going to finish setting the containers up. See you tomorrow."

Rita sighed. "Fine, but I think it is right up your alley."

"I have enough work here." Niiva kept walking back to the packing area.

Tubers were the harvest of the day. They were eaten by every Rrassic she had ever met. Niiva went over each container and made sure that they weren't shifting. An unstable load could wreck a shipment.

She was on the twelfth cargo container when her supervisor approached. "Niiva, you have missed the last shuttle to the city . . . again."

Niiva looked around and then checked her chronometer. "Oh. I guess I have a long walk ahead of me. Sorry, Supervisor Mreth."

The Sthik-Rrassic gave her a calm look. The Sthik were always calm, it was what made them such great supervisors for alien races.

"It is fine. Tomorrow is your day off anyway, but for today, take the cycle."

She frowned. "That is yours."

"Yes, but I am here late tonight to send out the shipment, and I will just sleep in my office."

She felt a guilty pang. "I can't."

"You can. So, get home, set the cycle to auto return, and if it gets here before I leave, I will take it home. The best chance of that happening is you leaving now."

Niiva finished tucking in the last of the tubers, and she sealed the unit. "Fine. I am leaving. Good evening, Supervisor Mreth, and I will see you in thirty-six hours."

Niiva bowed to her supervisor and was a little surprised when he walked her to the equipment garage where the cycle was kept. "You know that tomorrow isn't my scheduled day."

"I am aware of it, but I am putting it into your file due to your propensity for working after hours." He smiled. "The recruiters are also going to be here tomorrow, and I am very happy with your work here, so it is best that you are not here when they arrive."

"Recruiters? For the new peacekeeping team?"

"Indeed. It is selfish of me, but I do not want you to be snatched away from me." He blinked. "From our facility."

She smiled. "I consider you a friend, Supervisor."

"And I consider you an asset. Now, you remember how to ride the cycle?"

"I do. Can you register me as an authorized driver?"

"I did it before I came to dismiss you for the night. You are cleared and registered to take the cycle wherever you like."

Niiva grabbed the handles and pushed the cycle out of the holding area. It was a large electric bike that had a computer that was smarter than the supercomputers of most nations. The bike was sized for the seven-foot Rrassic, but it could be driven by a human if she knew what she was doing.

Niiva hopped up and straddled the bike below the seat. She powered it up and pulled on her helmet. Mreth kept it on hand for the humans who needed to make quick runs to other harvesters for staffing support. Niiva used the bike about once a month.

Mreth waved her off, and in the rear screen, she could see him returning to the warehouse.

She revved the cycle and settled onto the bike seat. The drive back to the city would take an hour. She couldn't approach the speed of the shuttle, but it was a fun ride.

Niiva mulled over Mreth's motives. Did he want to hide her from the job or from the Rrassic? She had noted a trend in his actions. When other Rrassic came to the warehouse, she was mysteriously sent off to another site where a Sthik was in charge.

She wondered what Mreth knew that he wasn't telling her. He had been hiding her since her last assessment. She was usually intent on her work, but even she had noticed that he was not letting her come into contact with other Rrassic. Her home was at the edge of the city, and she left before dawn to catch the shuttle out to her worksite. On her days off, she usually just booked in to get her hair done and a massage, sleeping the rest of the day. She socialized at work. Days off were for resting.

The lights of the city were ahead of her, and she leaned into the controls to increase to the edge of legal speed. The acceleration sent frissons of excitement through her, but she had to throttle down as she began to drive past pedestrians.

Her timing could have been better. She had just gotten to an intersection as the indicator changed when a drunk woman staggered into her path. The screech of the sudden stop made the woman flinch, and she stumbled back, falling off her heels and onto her ass.

Niiva sighed and stopped the cycle. She got up and walked around the bike to lift the woman to her feet, but two Regiz-Rrassic got there before her.

"You are not allowed to socialize with the females, human." One of them growled low.

The woman looked at the two males she was with and immediately went limp again.

The other asked, "Did you hit her with that cycle? What are you doing on one anyway?"

She frowned, but they couldn't see it. She was wearing the helmet, and it hid her from view. Her body was similarly concealed in a boiler suit that also masked her curves.

"I was working overtime and needed to get back to the city. The use of the cycle was authorized. Why weren't you looking out for your companion when she was obviously inebriated?" It was second nature to go on the attack.

The Regiz snarled at her, and one left their giggling lady with his friend, and he stalked toward her. "Who are you to accuse me of neglect?"

A new voice entered their little conversation. "*She's* one of the humans, Rokan. Use your fucking nose."

A solo Regiz walked up to her and bowed. "I saw the incident, and she fell on her own ass. May I assist you home?"

Niiva shook her head. "Thank you, but no. I am a little done with Rrassic males tonight."

She turned and got back on the cycle, steering it around the grouping and heading for the safety of her home.

Niiva activated the return function and left the cycle to travel on its own with her helmet tucked under the seat. She walked up the steps, and when she was inside her home, she groaned with relief. Going out and coming home was the tensest part of her day.

She opened the closure of her suit, kicked off her shoes, and walked to the bathroom for a shower and to release her breasts from the binding fabric that she used to keep them out of the way. Her job required a lot of lifting and reaching, and double Ds just didn't make it easy for her. Tying them down was painful, but it increased her range of motion.

Her shower was amazingly wonderful. She massaged her sore flesh and debated whether or not to masturbate that evening. It had been a tense day, and the release would be welcome, but the pheromones that she would give out might gain her some attention if she forgot to shower in the morning. Smiling, she reached between her thighs and circled her clit. She was in the shower now, so might as well kill two birds with one stone.

Argo walked to the peacekeeper dispatch office and headed to his desk. He brought up the registration number of the cycle he had seen and the list of registered users. Today, there was only one human registered for the operation of that cycle. Niiva Dollard. He brought up her stats, and he blinked. It couldn't be the same woman. No way would he have missed those curves.

He checked through the attendance logs at the harvesting and packaging centre, but everyone else had taken the shuttle home. Where the hell had her breasts gone?

He drummed his fingers on the table and got her ident number. He was scheduled to be in the harvest areas doing recruitment tomorrow. He would meet up with this shapeshifter then.

Her attitude had been amusing. She had stood up to the Hunters as if she expected to win the fight. There was nothing in her file to indicate that she was capable of hand-to-hand combat, but she had been willing to berate the Rrassic around her into submission. That amused him. She had a lot of fire, and if her file information was correct, she was stunning.

Idly, he opened up her medical file and was stuck looking at a blank page. There was no record of her last assessment or the one before that. Was the scent he had caught that of a human in heat? It was sweet and hot at the same time. But, if she was in heat, why didn't her supervisor send her in? Even Sthik could tell when a female was in season, even if they didn't want to do anything about it.

The next morning, Argo was standing in front of the workers at the harvesting centre, and one person was missing.

"Supervisor Mreth, where is Niiva Dollard?"

The supervisor cleared his throat. "She has been working overtime, so I granted her an extra day of rest."

Argo was more suspicious than he had been when he arrived, and as he went through and interviewed the women, looking for signs that they would be suited to law enforcement and asking them one pertinent question. Every woman at the harvesting facility had the same answer when asked, "Who among the women working here would be an excellent peacekeeper?" Every single woman answered, "Niiva."

The dark look that he gave to the supervisor promised further follow-up on how things had been handled. "I assume you have had a hand in her medical records as well?"

If it were possible for a Sthik to pale, Mreth would have.

Argo checked his chronometer and made a quick calculation. "Right. Sevos, Makrink, I will meet you back at the office. I have one last harvester to interview before this day is done."

They nodded.

Supervisor Mreth raised his hand. "Can't we keep her?"

Argo frowned. "If she is more suited to our work than yours . . . no, you can't."

The Sthik slumped his shoulders in defeat.

Argo got on his cycle and drove back to the city. He had a human to interview.

Chapter Two

The auto massager had finished with her an hour ago, and now, Niiva was hanging around her apartment wearing a loose skirt, matching shirt, and no bra. This was definitely the way to relax.

She waved the vid to the next selection and slouched on the couch with her hair loose around her. She giggled and watched the cartoons as they cavorted on the projected screen.

She was enjoying the day off, but because it wasn't on the schedule, she didn't have any of her favourite activities booked.

The knock at her door came as a bit of a surprise.

She grunted as she wedged herself off the couch and went to the door. She opened the door to a Regiz-Rrassic. "Hello?"

His mane of golden hair seemed to puff up, and his golden skin appeared to darken. "You are Niiva Dollard?"

"I am. Who are you?" There was something familiar about him. "Oh, wait. I saw you the other day."

His nostrils flared, and his eyes darkened. "I need to interview you for the position of peacekeeper."

She blinked. "What?"

"Your harvesting group was selected for interviews today, so as you are not at work, it was necessary to come to you. May I enter your domicile?"

She nodded and stepped back. "Please come in. Can I get you some tea?"

He nodded. "Yes, please. That would be welcome."

Niiva smiled and waved for him to take a seat. "I will just be a moment."

To say that he was stunned was an understatement. She was striking. Her hair was a tawny wave down her back, her eyes were a piercing green, and her figure was all curves. The shirt she was wearing lifted up slightly and exposed her waist, while the heavy sway of her breasts hypnotized him.

Her measurements were as recorded in the archive, but now that he saw them in action, he couldn't imagine how she hadn't been kept in the city or the Breeder quarters.

He inhaled deeply, and another punch to his groin occurred. She was either very receptive, or his nose was deceiving him in the cruellest way.

She returned and set a cup of tea down in front of him. The gesture gave him an unobstructed view into her shirt, and he had to jerk his gaze to one side. *Damn.*

When he looked away, she glanced down and quickly stood so that her neckline wasn't in full view. "So, what did you want to interview me for?"

"We are assembling a peacekeeping force, which includes humans. Toward that end, we are looking for human females who are willing to undergo the training to act as ambassadors of sorts to ease the conflicts that occur on Imrahl."

She nodded. "I am content as a harvester."

"The decision isn't yours to make. If you are suitable for this new assignment, you will change your occupation."

Niiva sighed. "I *like* working as a harvester and packager. I used to work on the family farm, and the labour is mostly the same. A lot of lifting and analyzing."

He nodded. "I gathered that when your supervisor gave

you today off so that you would not be there for the inter-view process."

"I did wonder about that." She didn't cross her arms over her breasts when she leaned forward to get her own tea. Ex-perience had taught her that it just brought attention to them.

"May I conduct the interview?"

She nodded, and he took out a flat tablet, setting it on the table.

"Please, keep all of your responses verbal."

She smiled. "I will. Yes, you may conduct the interview."

"Excellent. Niiva Dollard, do you consider yourself competent?"

"I do."

"Do you know your strength level?"

She frowned. "I don't know about the level, but I can comfortably lift my own weight or slightly above it."

He raised his brows in response to that. "Do you have a strong moral sense?"

"Yes."

"Do you have any formal combat training?"

"No. Nothing formal."

"Are you sexually receptive right now?"

The question caught her off guard. "What?"

"Are you sexually receptive right now?"

"Not that I am aware of."

He nodded. "Do you consider yourself to have fast reflexes?"

"I do."

"Do you consider yourself able to manage most vehicles on Imrahl?"

"I definitely do."

"Why would your supervisor keep you from applying for this position?"

"I believe he likes that I do half of his job as well as the job of two harvesters. And I can spot and destroy local predators. It means we don't have to scream for him when they come in on a shipment."

He nodded. "Good. There is just one more thing."

"What?"

"I need you to answer the receptivity question at a medical centre. Your scent is indicating that you are exceedingly receptive right now, but I am not going to make a judgment based on my own opinion."

She frowned. "Now?"

"Now. I will wait while you get some shoes on."

Niiva blinked. "Right. Okay. Just get it over with."

She finished her tea and put her sandals on. There was no sense in putting on undergarments. She really didn't care who saw what.

"Are we walking?"

"No, we will take my cycle."

She bit her lip and nodded. "Right. Lead the way."

"What has amused you?"

"Oh. Nothing."

When she settled on the back of the cycle and wrapped her arms around him for balance, he stiffened up. He gave her a dark glance but moved the cycle through the city streets at a sedate pace. It was probably for the best. One jolt of speed and her skirt would be up around her hips.

She watched the world go by as he drove. A few of the Rrassic on the sidewalks stared at them, but a quick glance down said it was because her skirt was creeping past mid-thigh.

They pulled up to the medical centre, and she released her grip, getting off the cycle with an audience of Rrassic watching her.

Argo looked at the men and scowled.

She finished settling her skirt back around her legs and waited. "Are we going in?"

He looked down at her, and he blinked slowly, as if stunned. "Yes, yes, we are. Just one thing."

He carefully reached out, and to her surprise, he tugged her shirt up from her shoulders.

She blushed. "How much cleavage was I showing?"

"Enough. Another woman wouldn't have been indecorous, but you were nearly indecent or issuing an invitation, which I am sure was not your intent."

She scowled. "It was not."

"There. Now, please, come with me."

She nodded and stepped forward, walking with him into the med centre. A quick glanced back showed the Rrassic gathered at the door. "Why are they back there?"

"My guess is that they are there to offer their services if you need help getting back on the cycle." There was a grim twist to his lips.

The Nool-Rrassic that came up to them smiled at Argo before looking at her. He looked startled, to say the least. "Niiva, what are you doing here?"

"I came under escort for an exam, Nedro."

Argo got his attention. "She is receptive, and yet, when I look up her file, it is completely blank. It is as if no testing has ever been done, but she remembers it being done. So, to correct this oversight, we are here to get her a full workup. Now."

Nedro nodded. "Niiva, please, come this way."

Argo raised his brows. "To make it clear, I will be in the room for all of her exams, even if I need to turn my back. We need those results."

Niiva frowned, but she knew exactly what kind of hard-asses the Rrassic could be about stuff like this.

She walked the halls with her two escorts until they went

into an exam room with all of the standard equipment for a full workup. Fortunately, with her current clothing choice, she only had to remove her shoes.

Nedro helped her up into the scan module and calibrated it for her height and weight. "Ready?"

She nodded, and he triggered the arc to begin its slow crawl up and down her body. Nothing physically touched her, but she could feel the contact of the scans under her skin. It measured the activity of her nervous system as well as her circulatory system.

While she was waiting for the scan, Argo was watching the progress of the unit. She used the opportunity to stare at him. It was rare that she got to see a proper Rrassic up close, other than Mreth.

Argo's jaw was wide, as was his neck. The thick highlights of golden hair were similar to her own tawny locks, but the undercurrent of black gave him a sinister appeal. His eyes were dark gold with feline pupils. With general assessment, he looked to be part weightlifter and part long-distance runner. There was a lot of strength in his body but grace as well. Most of the Regiz-Rrassic shared a similar body type, but Niiva was fairly sure that she could pick Argo out of a crowd of them.

"You have mild bruising around your breast tissue," Nedro murmured.

"Yeah, I was a little vicious with the wrap last week. It left a mark."

Argo stepped forward. "You are injured?"

She scowled. "No. It is a soft-tissue bruise. It will heal in a few days. You can't even see it."

Nedro spoke to him. "The compression bandages that she uses for breast restraint can cause capillary damage as well as minor damage to the muscles surrounding the breasts, but she does insist on wearing them."

Niiva frowned. "Hey, isn't there such a thing as Nool-patient confidentiality?"

Argo shook his head. "Not when it involves your safety or comfort."

She raised her brows, grabbed her shirt, and pulled it up, exposing her breasts. "Fine. Find the bruising."

Nedro's expression was shocked, but Argo took up the challenge. He stepped toward her and cupped her breasts in each hand, examining them carefully, running his finger along the right underside and pressing gently.

She couldn't help it. She flinched. On the left side, he found the small spot and pressed it, just near her underarm.

His hands were huge, but her breasts didn't quite fill them. She looked up into his eyes, and she tried to keep her bravado up. "Right. So, what do you win?"

He smiled, and his thumbs moved to graze her nipples. "I believe I have received my prize. So, breast support is necessary for you. More than you have received to date."

She blushed and dropped her shirt, letting his hands support the hem. "The undergarments that I have been offered to date tend to cantilever my breasts out at a weird angle. I look like a rain shelter for small creatures. I also can't see my feet."

He smiled, and his thumbs continued their slow caress. "I can imagine that would make things awkward. We will seek out a solution."

"Fine. I think Nedro wants to continue with the scans now. You have proved your point."

He withdrew his hands and stepped back.

Nedro sighed and started doing blood, saliva, and tissue samples.

After the saliva swab, she had to ask. "So, how did you find the bruising?"

"Heat. Recovering tissue is hotter than the tissue around

it due to increased blood flow." He took the report of the body scan from Nedro and used his tablet to copy it.

Nedro sighed. "It was a favour to Mreth. It is rare that he gets a strong and competent worker. I didn't think that one would make a difference."

Argo raised his brows. "We all know that one can make a difference. That is what this project is based on."

Nedro nodded. "Right. Of course. Yes, she is receptive, almost dangerously so. I will file my report with the overseer's office and wait for a reply."

"We will wait here."

Niiva sighed, put on her shoes, and went on to the next rounds of tests that verified her physical fitness.

Argo went quiet when she was doing the strength tests.

He asked Nedro, "Is that normal?"

"No, it is why Mreth wants to keep her. There aren't any of her people who are registering that kind of untrained power."

Niiva was leaning against the machine when Argo got his reply. He nodded.

"Right. We have an appointment with the overseer. Nedro, please, forward all of the results to my unit. Niiva, come with me."

"Why?"

"Because you are about to engage in a change of state and that is going to require authorization for you to keep any kind of occupation aside from your Breeder status."

Niiva blinked. "Isn't that status negotiable?"

He gave her a long, slow look as he took her hand. "No."

Niiva had to admit that having a guy say no to her was sort of a turn-on, not that she needed the help.

Chapter Three

Hearing a Rrassic growl at others of his kind was a little odd. The low growl had started when they left the med centre, and when the gathered men converged on her, Argo snarled and gnashed his teeth at them.

She was tucked in front of him this time, and they roared off to the main administration building without hesitation.

Argo was in a definite mood, and the erection pressed against her backside might have had something to do with it.

When they pulled up at the administration building, his arms were humming with tension.

He lifted her off the bike before he dismounted, and she took the hint and entered the building a few steps ahead of him.

She felt slight touches on her back to direct her left and right. They were silent in the lift, and as they approached the receptionist's desk, she got to her feet with wide eyes and got the overseer's door open.

Argo escorted her into the overseer's office, and he was huffing slightly. "Overseer, this is the female that I sent you the report on."

The overseer looked at her, and he smiled slightly. "I see. You are not wrong, she is putting out a powerful scent."

Niiva frowned. "That doesn't sound very polite."

The receptionist shook her head. "It just means that you are ovulating or, at the very least, smell like a woman who is sexually aroused. I am Isabella, by the way."

The woman stuck her hand out, and there was a silver band around her wrist. The second band was on the other arm, and a matching band was around her throat.

Niiva shook the woman's hand. "Niiva Dollard."

"Pleased to meet you. This is Iktabi, the overseer of Imrahl operations."

Argo growled. "Enough of the pleasantries."

The growl got Iktabi on his feet, and his wings flared out. It seemed to be enough of a threat display that Argo came back to his senses.

"Apologies, Isabella. I did not mean to growl."

Isabella smiled sweetly. "It is fine. I understand your distress. Iktabi gets cranky when he is horny as well."

Niiva stifled a giggle as the overseer gave his secretary a dark glance. Isabella gave him a beatific smile in return.

Iktabi folded his wings in and returned to his chair. "So, the problem is that she is highly receptive but has no mate or males courting her but is attracting all and sundry and would make an excellent peacekeeper. Am I caught up?"

Argo nodded.

Iktabi looked her over, and an amused smile turned up the corners of his mouth. "I can see the appeal. Argo, are you interested?"

"I am."

"Niiva, are you interested in Argo, even as a short-term lover?"

Niiva looked at the Regiz, and she smiled. "Keep talking."

Argo looked surprised, and she felt his weight shift toward her.

Isabella smiled. "I will get her a spot in the Breeder compound and have her possessions moved. Niiva, you don't socialize much, do you?"

"No. It is really not my thing."

"Good. Lianne and Sorrok can do a battle-capability assessment tomorrow and see what kind of training you need."

Argo chipped in. "She requires additional breast support."

Niiva went scarlet, and she slapped him in the arm.

Isabella smiled. "There are options for that as well. The workout gear that the tailors have worked on is adaptive for most sizes, and the straps that secure the band in place are very comfortable, no matter what the issues."

Niiva arched her brow. "Will I be able to see my feet?"

Isabella looked her over. "Probably not, but you won't bounce in two directions when you move. They are like tailored sports bras, only they start with a band, and the wraps keep them where you want them."

Niiva caught the bewildered looks that the men were giving each other, and she smiled. "I think that might work. So, tomorrow?"

"Mid-morning. I will have your escort pick you up."

Argo scowled. "I will take her."

Iktabi gave him a look. "You have a job, Peacekeeper. We will try and get you into her entourage, but if you are needed elsewhere, she will travel with others."

Niiva frowned. "Do I get a say in any of this?"

Iktabi nodded. "You can choose your mate. Aside from that, we have the right to allow our men to court and seduce you within reason. It was explained to you when you were assigned to your job."

Niiva scowled. "Yes, but I never thought it would apply to me."

Iktabi suddenly got a suspicious look on his features. He opened a file and displayed it. On one side of a desk, Isabella was working at a terminal; on the other, Niiva was sitting and looking queasy. With a sly move, Isabella took the chip that had come out of the machine, and she slipped it under her desk. A second chip was printed and put in the band that Niiva wore out of the office.

Isabella blushed, and Niiva stared at her. "I remember you now. You said that I wouldn't have to worry about the men coming after me right away. Thank you."

Isabella took a few steps back toward Iktabi. "I may have forgotten to mention Niiva on the list of females that I gave you. She was in a good position doing good work."

Argo stared at Isabella. "Did you delete her medical records?"

Isabella's eyes widened as she was reeled backward by an invisible force. "No, but that would have been a good idea. I just wanted to slow her discovery."

Isabella fell into Iktabi's lap, and he wrapped his arms around her. He whispered into her ear for a few moments, and her cheeks got redder and redder.

Niiva looked at Argo, and she cocked her head. "How do you feel about casual sex?"

His throat worked, and no decipherable sounds came out.

Iktabi leaned forward and tapped rapidly on his tablet with the hand that wasn't holding his female. "The reservation at the Breeders quarters has been received; you will be taken to a set of rooms when you arrive."

Isabella cleared her throat. "I am ordering the move for your possessions. They will arrive in the next four hours."

Niiva nodded. "Fine. If I can't be a harvester, when I can start working at something else?"

Isabella smiled. "When you finish your training as a peacekeeper, so it is up to you."

"What do I need to know?"

Isabella looked up from her screen. "You are going to need to know the laws that govern both species on Imrahl, be physically capable of subduing a Rrassic, and conversant with all the vehicles that are in use on our streets."

Niiva nodded. "Okay, so I just need the laws and a few vehicles. Maybe some speed moves."

Iktabi looked at her with amusement. "It takes a bit of strength to fight a Rrassic."

"May I borrow your mate?" Niiva smiled.

Iktabi released Isabella, and the other human walked over to her. With a slight bending of the knees, Niiva lifted the receptionist and turned to face Iktabi. "I have strength."

Iktabi's eyes widened. "Apparently so."

Isabella cleared her throat. "Can you put me down now?"

Niiva set Isabella back on her feet. "There you go."

"Thank you. That is impressive. You didn't quiver or anything."

Niiva smiled. "I lift for a living. I don't have a lot of fine control though. Just strength moves."

Iktabi looked to Argo. "You know of this?"

Argo nodded. "I watched during the testing. She could probably flip one of us if she had the advantage of leverage."

The overseer nodded and smiled. "You two can be on your way. Niiva Dollard, thank you for your cooperation."

Isabella was back in his lap, and Niiva waved a small farewell as she left the office.

Teasing Argo might have not been her brightest idea. He was a looming presence behind her while she waited for the lift, and she could feel the heat radiating from his body.

She dragged in a shaking breath and tried to ignore her body like she did every day. It was difficult to feel a constant pulse of desire and be unable to act on it. If she was right, she was being given the chance to ride a few of the Rrassic. She didn't want to pass up the chance, but if she started with Argo, would she want to keep moving through the ranks?

Standing next to him in the lift was torture. It was a handful of seconds, but the proximity was working on her like foreplay. She was every caricature of a farmer's daughter.

Her body was ready the moment she turned her mind to it. Resisting her own impulses was the hardest thing to do.

When the doors opened, Argo led the way back to the cycle. She cleared her throat. "Do you want me in front or behind?"

He gave her a dark look. "Behind me. If I get my arms around you, I will be hard pressed to keep my mind on the road."

She nodded and licked her lips. "Fine. You get on first, and I will settle behind you."

He nodded, his jaw tense. He settled on the cycle, and she slipped on behind him, wrapping her arms around his waist. His pulse quickened when she pressed her breasts against his back. She heard him cursing in High Rrassic as he activated the cycle and they entered traffic. She kept her head pressed against his back and her thighs pressed to the backs of his while he took them through the city and over to the Breeder compound. When he paused, and she heard a voice asking for her ident, she extended her left arm and looked at the man so he could compare the scan of her features with the real thing.

The Sthik-Rrassic looked at her and nodded with a slight smile. "Welcome to the compound, Niiva Dollard. Your possessions are on the way."

She nodded and smiled slightly. "Thank you."

Argo gave him a look, and the barrier was swiftly lowered. The cycle carried them through the expanse of the drive to the large, sprawling building. Out front, Argo parked, and she quickly disentangled herself from him, sliding off the seat and pulling her skirt straight so that the slick moisture from her thighs was camouflaged. Underwear would have been a good idea, but she hadn't been planning on leaving the house.

She looked at Argo as he disabled the cycle. She hadn't

been planning for a lot of things.

Chapter Four

By the time they reached the quarters assigned to her at the main security desk, a wave of bots was behind them, carrying her wardrobe and her tiny collection of possessions.

"You use bots for moving?"

Argo nodded. "They don't get sidetracked with scents."

She nodded and stood aside as the bots zipped back and forth with her possessions.

Argo checked, and when there were no more incoming bots, he eased her around the corner, into her new quarters.

She whistled softly. "This is larger than the home I grew up in."

He smiled. "The space is designed for your comfort. All of the amenities that your apartment had are contained here as well."

She didn't have a lot of stuff, so as the bots finished, they filed out, closing the door behind them.

She cleared her throat. "So, there is a massage unit?"

He nodded. "Of course."

Niiva cleared her throat. "Could you show me? I am feeling a little tense."

Argo gave her a slow, raking look. It covered her from head to toe and let her know that he had a thing for breasts and hips. Also, her hair got a lot of attention.

Niiva decided to make a move. A quick glance at his groin said he was exceedingly interested, so she stepped toward him, placing a hand on the black fabric that covered his chest.

"So, since I am authorized to take a lover, and you are authorized to be that lover. Would you care to demonstrate the finer points of the Rrassic physique?" She slid her hand up his chest and touched his neck where his pulse was thundering.

He pulled her to him with hands around her waist. "You want me?"

She nodded. "I do."

"Then, you shall have me." He lifted her, and she wrapped her legs around his waist. His groan let her know that it had been the right move.

He walked with her through the empty space of her living room and through an archway to her bedroom. He knew his way around the Breeders quarters, but she was relieved rather than irritated. At least he knew what humans were like.

She kissed him and was a little surprised at the rough texture of his tongue when he slid it into her mouth. Niiva wove her fingers through his hair and deepened the kiss as he moved his grip from her waist to her thighs and then under her skirt. When he found her slick and wet, he paused.

He pulled his head back and shivered as he swallowed when his finger grazed the soft folds that were slick with invitation.

She shivered and leaned toward his neck, biting softly.

He growled. "Are you attached to this clothing?"

"Not particular—" The sound of shredding fabric filled the room. She was naked and her clothing in tatters in seconds.

He looked down at her and grinned, showing most of his very sharp teeth. "Perfect."

He laid her back on the bed and opened the closures on his trousers, freeing his cock. She didn't have much of a chance to admire the gold length before he was on her and inside her.

The pressure of his entrance continued until she couldn't take him any further. Argo shifted and moved his hips rapidly, holding his body away from hers while the only place they connected was between her thighs.

Sweat coated her skin, and she bent her legs to press her feet flat to the bed in order to push him in deeper. The pressure and friction were what she was after, and as they pounded together, she reached between them to touch her clit. A few frenzied circles of building tension and she gasped and grunted as her body contracted around him.

Argo groaned and held himself against her as her body shook in long pulses. She held still while he pressed against her again and again until he finally shuddered to completion.

She was a little disappointed. She had hoped for more contact.

Argo closed his eyes for a moment, and when he opened them, there was a light in his gaze. He slowly pulled out of her and peeled his clothing off, starting at his tunic. When the black fabric was discarded, the muscles of his torso gleamed under the gold hide that the Regiz were so proud of.

The more clothing he removed, the less he resembled a human. Niiva blushed as the sight started her arousal all over again.

When he was wearing a feral grin and nothing else, he crept toward her, covering her from head to toe as he kissed her.

She met the slow and careful thrust of his tongue with her own, and when her body started giving her orders, she arched against him, rubbing her breasts against his chest.

He lowered his torso until he was pinning her to the bed. She settled for a slow squirm against him while she tried to touch as much of his back as she could. His body was hard muscle wrapped in gold velvet. If she could touch him constantly, she would.

The erection against her thigh was the same soft texture, and if he hadn't been pinning her down, she would have been trying to coax him inside her again.

He reached out and eased her hands away from their death-grip in the muscular groove of his back and pinned her hands next to her head. The restriction worked on her body, and she was on the edge of growling herself. Instead of a growl, a whimper came from her throat when the arousal became desperation.

She felt his lips curve against her in a feral grin. The sound had been what he was waiting for.

He moved quickly. One moment he was on top of her, and then, he had reared back, flipped her over, and was pressing her into the sheets from behind.

His thighs were pressing hers apart, and his fingers were woven with hers, holding her in place.

Niiva could feel the blind head of his cock seeking entrance. The slow slide of heat against her had her shifting her hips to try and get it where she wanted, no, needed it to be.

His voice was dark as he whispered against her neck, "Do you want me?"

She hissed and turned her head to one side. "Yes." It came out as another hiss.

"Do you want me inside you, as deep and hard as you can take me?"

She nodded, and he nipped the edge of her ear. "Use your words."

She was beginning to hate that smug tone. "I do want you hard and deep."

He shifted his hips, and his cock teased her opening. "Thank you for the invitation, Niiva. I am going to honour it."

He moved inward, and she felt tears leak from her eyes in relief.

He was in control, but his chest rubbed against her as he moved, and soon, he released her hands to rear up and explore her skin with a lot of attention given to her backside. He really seemed to like to fondle and stroke the globes of her ass as he drove into her. His hands gripped and kneaded her ass as he pounded into her with attention to every moan and murmur that escaped her.

Her fingers dug into the sheets under her, and she pushed upward to rock back against him. The hands on her ass suddenly moved to brace himself as her back was now his balance platform. He grunted and held himself inside her while he wrapped an arm around her waist and pulled her up and onto her knees.

She grinned and locked her elbows.

He rubbed his chest against her back, and she rocked back against him, sliding her sheath around him. *Oh, yeah.*

Niiva rocked onto him, and he gradually thrust back until they were slamming into each other with ferocity. His low growls sent coils of excitement through her, and she was about to cum when she felt his breath against her neck and a spike of pain shot through her system, providing a radiant burn that flashed through her.

She tried to jerk away from his teeth, but his arms held her fast. He slid a hand down her belly and rubbed her clit while rocking into her. She shivered and held still as her body recovered from the shock and her frenzied state roared back to life.

A series of soft cries came from her throat, and the controlled motions inside and outside her folds rocked her until light exploded behind her eyes and her voice froze on a silent scream.

Her entire focus turned inward to the hot, throbbing invader inside her, the relentless touch on her clit moving in slick circles, and her body squeezing down and clutching at him, milking his cock.

He groaned, and his teeth shifted slightly. She smelled her own blood, and then, a low series of grunts and growls announced his release.

The hum of a med kit against the side of her neck brought her out of her daze. She was lying on her side, her thighs were sticky, and the scent of sex filled the air. The low throb deep inside her let her know that it had been less than three minutes since he had been inside her.

The hot throb of her neck gradually cooled as the small abrasion regenerator worked to close the surface wounds on her skin.

When the med kit was removed, she turned to watch Argo moving about the space. He was tense. There was no doubt about that. He went through a doorway and returned with a folded cloth in his hands. She turned to her back and parted her knees, guessing at what he was going to do. He met her gaze and then looked away.

His voice was low and hoarse. He removed the cum from her thighs and said, "I apologize. I lost my head."

She smiled at the cool pressure on her thighs, and then, she pushed past him. "Excuse me."

He grabbed her arm. "Is something wrong?"

"I need to use the lav." She smiled and tried to walk naturally, but there was a bit of a wobble. She hadn't had this kind of an encounter for a while.

"Leave the door open."

She sighed and took care of herself; then, she pressed a cooling cloth to her groin. A quick look in the mirror showed pink discolouration where he had bitten her. It would be completely faded by the following day, but right now, she shivered at the memory of the hot, wet, sharp pain. Glancing down, her nipples were drawn tight, and she winced at the proof of her unstoppable libido.

Niiva sighed.

Argo waited for her at the doorway. "What is wrong?"

She walked up to him and into his arms. His hug was immediate. "You would think that with all the trouble they went through to clone me and copy my memories, they could have balanced my hormones a little better."

He froze. "What?"

"The human women here are all clones. Some of us know, some don't, and if we do, we keep it to ourselves."

He didn't say anything.

"It's fine, Argo. I know. I am missing two scars, and I wasn't on my hormone cocktail when I came to. Trust me, there is no way that I would have simply stopped treatment unless it wasn't known that I was getting treatment."

He ran his hands up and down her back. "This day has gotten far more complicated than I imagined."

She lifted her head, looking at him and feeling the throb in her neck. "I think I can second that remark. Can we just have a lie-down?"

He nodded with a smile. "We can. I just need to make a call."

She sighed and knew that their one afternoon together had gotten more complicated than she could imagine.

Chapter Five

Whatever she had been expecting, a full medical team of Nool with diagnostic equipment was not part of it, nor was the sight of Iktabi and Isabella. There was also a hooded figure with them, but he didn't speak.

Niiva wore her favourite robe, and Argo was wearing his uniform. While she was still very interested in having another run at his body, she accepted that this wasn't the time.

Isabella took her by the hand and pulled her aside. "Argo mentioned that you think you are a clone."

Niiva gave Isabella a bland look. "I am missing scars; I had no trace of my hormone therapy in my system. My normal libido started to build slowly, and when I worked physically, I could ignore it. The moment that stopped, it came roaring back as the extra testosterone and adrenaline had nowhere to go."

Isabella blinked. "Oh. Oh . . ."

"Right. So, the moment that my routine was altered, the libido came roaring back. At home, I had been on therapy for the last five years. It was a relief to my family. My behaviour was getting wilder as I tried to work off my desperation."

The man with the hood had been at the edge of their conversational space. Niiva had felt a cool wash in her thoughts, and as she finished explaining to Isabella, he turned and walked off toward where Iktabi and Argo were conversing.

Niiva grimaced. "I think he is squealing on me."

Isabella patted her shoulder. "I think that he needed to

make sure that it wasn't a conspiracy theory and that you hadn't told anyone."

"Fine. Is that one of the Saya-Rrassic?"

Isabella smiled. "He is."

"Do they really have three eyes?"

A voice called out from the other room. "I do!"

Isabella laughed.

Niiva blushed and called out, "Thank you!"

There was a laugh from the men, and Niiva asked Isabella, "Can I make you some tea?"

"Sure. Can you find your way around the kitchen?"

Niiva wrinkled her nose. "We will find out."

Argo looked at the overseer. "Things got out of hand."

Iktabi nodded. "You had sex."

"We did. Yes. And then we mated."

The Dorbin-Rrassic's brows rose high. "You did what?"

"We mated. She was so responsive, so perfect, and my impulses took over."

Iktabi covered his eyes. "Did you get her consent?"

"For the sex, yes. Mating, no."

The overseer scowled. "That is a breach of protocol."

"I know. All I can say is that she smelled like my mate."

The Saya-Rrassic joined them. "She knows, and she has no doubts. The difference in her body is apparent, and she knows it."

Iktabi nodded. "Isabella knows as well. She has adapted to it."

The Saya lifted his head, smiled, and yelled out, "I do!"

There was feminine laughter from the other room, and Niiva called out, "Thank you!"

The Saya smiled. "You have a very desirable mate, Argo."

Argo felt a flash of jealousy before he calmed it. "How do

you know?"

"I did an examination of her mind. Overseer, there is a measurable difference between her mind imprint and what she has now."

Iktabi frowned. "Explain."

"The initial imprint was calm and sedate with a good work ethic. Her current sense of self is an awareness of her body in a riot. Her hormones and adrenaline surge uncontrollably and cause a dramatically increased libido. She recognized the sensation from her adolescence, and that is why she was surprised to wake without it. By the time her body caught up to the mind imprint, she was already working at the harvest centre. She was able to focus that attention and aggression into her work."

Iktabi winced. "What are the chances that there are others like her out there?"

"Slim. She is exotic even among her family group. There is a tale of one great-grandmother with the same issue and seventeen children."

Iktabi blinked, and Argo looked toward the other room with a sense of possessive smugness. "How many twins?"

Saya checked the memory that he had just obtained. "Three pairs."

Argo wanted to rush in and find out if Niiva was already pregnant. His conscious mind knew it was a near impossibility, but his instincts said that she had been fertile during their coupling.

Iktabi put out his hand. "Without her consent, if she has conceived, this might be your only offspring. She will be encouraged to seek out another."

Argo growled low. "No."

"You have no say in it. You have jumped the gun here, as my mate likes to say. We have these rules in place for a reason."

Argo snarled. "Does she know?"

The Saya shook his head. "She doesn't. She knows the humans were cloned to be here, she doesn't know why."

Iktabi cocked his head. "Argo, part of your disciplinary action will be to tell her and take her on a tour of the gestation facility."

Argo frowned. "I don't have clearance."

Iktabi lifted his tablet and made a few entries. "You do now."

The Nool medics came forward. "We are ready to do the analysis."

Argo nodded. "I will get her."

The medic held up his hand. "I will retrieve her."

Iktabi put his hand on Argo's arm to stop him from following.

Argo watched the Nool bring Niiva from the other room, and he smiled slightly when she winked at him as she passed. It seemed that nothing could make an impact on her mood.

The scanners were focused on her head and lower abdomen.

A light chime got everyone's attention. The three Nool medics focused on the monitor, and one of them looked back at her with a smile. "I will get the canisters from the transport vehicle."

Argo was next to the team in a second. "Canisters?"

The Nool grinned. "She released two eggs, and you caught them."

Niiva blinked. "I am pregnant?"

Argo came over to her and whispered in her ear. He explained about the Rrassic, the war, and their desperate attempts to build an army using the next generation. They had the skills to develop clones at a rapid pace but recreating the same beings over and over wasn't an option. They needed to bring their race forward, and that meant blending with others in order to create a variety that could survive and thrive on Rrassia. Humans were a close match, and mixing some Rrassic DNA in during the cloning process had created ideal mates for the Rrassic warriors, chosen for their desirable characteristics.

Niiva's normally cheerful demeanour darkened. "You are taking the babies."

He nodded. "We will go to the gestation centre, and you can visit them as they develop, but the goal is to gain as many embryos from human women as we can, that means that continuing a pregnancy is not a desirable outcome. Do not worry, we grew you, we can grow our children."

She frowned, and one of the Nool who was watching her scans called out a warning. She punched out, and Argo staggered backward, clutching his jaw.

Iktabi and Isabella were staring in shock.

Argo looked to them and said, "Combat training first and then the gestation centre. I want her calmed down before she is around all those canisters."

Niiva's fury faded and she cracked a smile. "It might not be a bad idea."

Argo exhaled. "Okay. So, you have a flash temper. Good to know."

The Nool with the canisters came back into the room, and he looked around cautiously. "What happened?"

Niiva smiled. "I was celebrating being pregnant. If you canister my little ones, I look forward to doing the same again at a later date."

Argo looked wary, and she smirked. "Serves you right."

Isabella chuckled.

Niiva looked at her. "Have you had this done?"

"Yes, my little girl is about this big now." Isabella held

her hands about two inches apart. "My son is smaller than my fingernail."

Iktabi put his arms around his mate, and Isabella stroked his arm.

The Nool prepared a sterile tray and the canisters at her side. Niiva babbled a little. "Are yours the oldest?"

Isabella shook her head. "No, Lianne and Sorrok's triplets are the oldest. Two boys and a girl, but the one that will be first decanted belong to Bree and Arix. She's another one with unusual characteristics."

Argo came over and took her hand. She held onto it with a lot of focus.

There was a slight twinge as the extraction procedure began, and in six minutes, it was over.

The canisters began to glow the moment that the tissue struck them. Signs of life or, at least, an energetic chemical reaction.

She exhaled slowly, and a cellular regenerator was pressed to her abdomen. "Is that it?"

The Nool nodded. "That is it. You likely won't cycle again for two months, but you will need to come in for scans every two weeks."

She frowned. "Why?"

Isabella cleared her throat. "The Rrassic part of the equation grow very quickly and are draining to maintain. This isn't a human pregnancy. The best place for the little ones and for us is to have them in the canisters, growing up to be big and healthy."

"How dangerous could it be?"

"Bree nearly died. Her system was being drained of every mineral and fat needed to build a body. She had an accelerated pregnancy, but it was a very good example of how bad things could go if not properly taken care of. We aren't human, our babies aren't human. Once you get your head around that, it is the best solution."

Niiva sighed and looked at the solution in the canisters. She couldn't even see the specks that were hers and Argo's.

"I can go visit them?"

"As often as your peacekeeper training allows," Argo whispered in her ear.

She nodded. "That starts tomorrow?"

"It does. They will come for you in the morning." Argo smiled.

Iktabi muttered something in High Rrassic. "Right. Argo, you are assigned to her as her mate and her trainer. Make sure that she doesn't hurt anyone too badly."

Isabella winked and left the room; Iktabi followed. The Nool took the hint, and as the overseer of Imrahl left the room, they gathered their things up and evacuated.

The Saya-Rrassic was the last one to leave. He paused and turned to them. "You are very well suited to each other in every way. Remember that when you drive each other crazy."

He bowed and left the room, closing the door behind him with a definite click.

Argo was standing with his arms around her, and she didn't remember when she had gone into his embrace. He exhaled. "This is not the way I thought my day was going to go."

She smiled slightly. "Regrets?"

"A few, but I will get over it."

She leaned back and rubbed her head against his collarbone. "I think I need a bath and a nap. I seem to recall that there is a rather large bathroom off the bedroom."

He squeezed her. "Lead the way."

Five minutes later the bath that seemed large enough for four was taken up with Niiva and Argo. She breathed in deeply, supported by his arms around her. "This was not how I thought my day was going to go either."

He slowly ran his hand down her thigh and back up again. "Regrets?"

She moved and sat across his lap, looking into his eyes. "A few, but I will get over it."

He leaned in to kiss her, and she met him halfway. Acrobatics could wait for another day. Tonight, she just wanted to relax. It had been quite the eventful afternoon.

Chapter Six

After a night in Argo's arms, they got up, had breakfast, and then went to the gym that had been set aside for training the human peacekeepers. So far, she was the second.

Lianne and Sorrok met them in the front hall, and when Niiva had collected her workout gear, they headed for the change room.

"It is so nice to see another woman in the peacekeepers. Are you excited to be training?"

Niiva was standing naked with the breast band in her hands trying to figure it out. "Um, I was sort of assigned this position. Don't worry. I can do the job."

Lianne took the band from her and turned it around. "When you have it settled, I will help you with the straps. That is the hardest part."

Niiva got the breast band settled and put on the wide-legged trousers that tied snugly around her waist.

Lianne held the straps in one hand. "May I?"

Niiva nodded. "Please."

Lianne clipped one side of the band and wrapped the strap to the opposite side on Niiva's back. Then, she ran another set of straps beneath the band to hold it against her ribs.

"How is that?"

Niiva looked at herself in the mirror, and she blinked. "It is really comfortable. Thanks."

She jumped up and down, and her breasts moved but didn't jolt or jiggle. "Very nice. I might get this to wear under my clothing."

Lianne grinned. "I have to admit, I am impressed that it provides that much containment. You have a lot of curves and even more muscle."

Niiva smiled. "I work physically for a living."

"That would do it."

"What is your occupation?"

Lianne wrinkled her nose. "I drive lifts at the port."

"Wow. That is a lot of fine-motor control."

"Thank you. Yes, it is." Lianne chuckled.

They left the change room and walked down the hall to the area where the arena was. Argo had briefed her on the way in. All the equipment that they needed to assess her was for Hunter use. That meant going into the open space where the Rrassic were and showing them what she could do.

"They are going to be watching, but don't worry. Argo will keep them in check."

"He won't have to. If I get my blood up, I can stop any of them that get grabby."

Lianne bit her lip. "Are you sure? The Rrassic are pretty strong."

The door opened in front of them, and they walked into the arena. "So am I."

Argo was standing wearing the same style of trousers that she was and nothing else. It was just the thing she needed to get her blood flowing.

He grinned and came toward her, extending his hand to her. "This way, Niiva. Your audience awaits."

He wasn't kidding. There were at least thirty Hunters at the edge of the arena, some seated, some standing, but all watching.

Niiva shrugged. She would do her job. That was why she was here.

Argo smiled. "Are you ready for this?"

"Let's start and see how far I get before I try and find a way out of these clothes." Her smile was wry, and his eyes flared in surprise.

"Right. Calibration for the combat simulator is first up."

Argo gestured to the machine that she was already slightly familiar with. Niiva settled her feet in the marked positions, and Argo lowered the bar onto her shoulders to the amused murmurs of her audience. This machine was going to determine the pushing strength in her legs. The readout was in front of her.

She lowered into a high crouch with the bar across her shoulders when Argo said, "Go!"

She pushed upward. It was too easy. "More."

She went down again, and the bar settled heavily against her.

"Go!"

She pushed up, and it was more difficult but not at her limit.

She looked to Argo and smiled. "A little bit more."

"I will never turn you down asking for more." He set the equipment, and when she was straining to stand up, he called, "Go!"

She pushed up and then dropped to the ground. The bar stopped a foot above her. She looked at the readout and grinned. They must have done something to her genes because lifting five hundred pounds should not have been possible.

Argo helped her to her feet, and he smiled. "Next, punching."

Lianne and Sorrok were engaged in some light warmups, but occasionally, they glanced her way as she was tested for punching, pulling, pushing, and kicking.

She leaned against Argo, drinking her water and watching the computer analyze her physical specs. "So, no living contact, huh?"

"Not until you learn to pull your punches, pet." He rubbed the back of her neck.

"Right, so simulations?"

"And form practice. You will be doing a lot of practice with form for combat poses."

She wrinkled her nose. "Okay. When do I start?"

"Now if you are not too tired."

Niiva put her water jug next to the dispenser. "I am ready if you are."

He extended his hand and led her to the mat where the other two were sparring. He showed her the first position and urged her to follow him.

After forty-five minutes of moving slowly and deliberately, she was shaking, covered in sweat, and still not sure she was doing it right.

Argo looked at her and smiled. "We are going to call it a day."

She bent over with her hands on her knees. "Good call."

All of her major muscle groups were trembling. The fine-motor control needed for martial art was new to her.

Her mate wrapped his arm around her waist and helped her back to the gender barrier that kept him out of the ladies' changing area. "I will be waiting for you in the front entryway."

She grunted. "I may be some time."

He grinned at her. "Take your time. There are hot showers, and they may help."

She made a face at him, and then, she straightened herself to walk into the change room. The top she was wearing was surprisingly easy to get off. She simply unsnapped the straps and pushed the tube down and off her body. It snagged on the trousers, so she untied them and pushed them away as well. Getting naked took a minute and a half, and when she had the bundle of clothing under her arm, she walked to the showers and set the temperature up as high as it would go.

Her skin was hot pink when she finally stepped out of the stall, but she felt like she was in control of her limbs again.

Her clothing was gone. Darn. She wanted to keep that top.

She returned to her locker and used her wristband to open it. Her clothing was just as she had left it. She pulled her underwear and then her clothing on, sliding her feet into her low shoes.

Her limbs were humming, and she had no idea when Lianne and Sorrok had left, but she didn't remember seeing them on the way out. She wished she could have observed their workout. It might have helped her with her positioning.

With a groan, she exited the change room, and true to his word, Argo was waiting for her.

He offered her his arm, and she took it. "You did well today, Niiva."

"Thanks. I probably shouldn't have shown off during the weightlifting."

"We will go and get something to eat, and I can tell you what I observed."

"Oh. Good. Make sure I am fed before you get too critical."

She grinned at him, and he gave her a wary smile. Keeping him on his toes was nice. From what the ladies used to talk about at the harvest centre, the Regiz were obsessed with curves and beauty. Argo had just hooked himself to a bit of a beast. She wondered how long it would be before he ran.

She felt her expression flicker as she thought about all the boyfriends that her energy and her libido had sent running. Having a girlfriend with a huge sexual appetite seemed like a man's dream, but when she could also pull a physical advantage, it was rather frightening. She wore them out, and they left.

They walked to the restaurant that was full of Rrassic. She paused. "Are you sure you want me in here?"

"Your biology is rather sedate today. I will risk it." He winked.

He held the door open for her, and she stepped inside. The entire restaurant went silent. Argo put his arm around her waist, and the server came over, bowing and escorting them to a booth.

Niiva groaned as her buttocks protested. "Okay, I definitely overdid it this morning."

He laughed, and when the server came up to them, he placed his order in High Rrassic. The Nool smiled, inclined his head, and headed off.

"What did you order?" She tried to get comfortable, but it was like her clothing was abrading her.

"Something to help you with muscle growth, and it has an analgesic effect on your species. That tuber that you were harvesting, it is the base of most of our meals, and it is a very useful item."

"Well, that explains why half of Imrahl's farms contain those tubers."

He smiled, and tea arrived. It was always tea on Imrahl. She had heard that there was coffee to be had in some of the human-run shops, but she had never been to one that served it. It was too bad. She missed coffee.

Argo poured the tea in tall tumblers and handed hers over. "Well, I have to say that I am extremely impressed with your workout today."

She blew on the tea. "Thank you. I know it was a disaster."

"It was not a disaster. Not everyone has the finesse for the moves of our combat practice. You do."

The last two words caught her by surprise. "I do? I fell down a lot."

"But you stayed up more and kept your strength in all your moves. That is key. If you do the moves without the power, it is just dancing." He smiled again.

She felt better. "Well, power is the one thing I can bring."

He nodded and reached out to squeeze her hand. "So I saw."

She nodded. "Does that bother you?" The words rushed out before she could stop them.

"Bother me?"

"Yes. With humans, it is common that the men are not precisely enamoured with physically intimidating women."

Argo blinked, and a slow smile crept over his lips. "You think I am intimidated?"

She sighed and sat back. "I don't know what to think, so I am drawing on my memory. Men used to be very enthusiastic at the beginning, but as the demands on them continued, they found other partners."

"You mean sex."

She felt her cheeks pink. "Yes."

"Your demanding nature is part of you. So far, you have indicated your interest and allowed me to choose the form that interest would take. It was a delightful dance, and I look forward to the music when it comes."

Niiva stared at him, looking for any nuance of deception in his features. There was nothing but some light amusement and a hint of memories of the day before.

She was still blushing when the food arrived, and while she felt like she was sitting at the kids' table, she reached out and took the eating prongs from the too-tall table.

Suddenly, the food that she had helped bring to the city took on a new nature as she began to eat. It was now a tool that was going to help her do her job, and if she were lucky, she would get to see the small specks that she and Argo had created so carefully the day before.

The gestation centre was the next thing on her list to make sure that the entire procedure hadn't just been a weird dream.

Chapter Seven

In the secure vehicle on the way to the gestation centre, Argo murmured to Niiva, "The only other human who knows is Isabella. Remember that."

She nodded and swallowed. "So, the reason for the accelerated development has to do with us as well as you."

"Correct."

"So, what happens when the children are born?"

"We raise them, or we hand them over to a creche. It is up to you."

A sense of panic filled her. "I never thought of being a mother."

"Do not worry. It has come on you suddenly, and no one will judge you for your lack of maternal feelings right now."

"Did you have a mother?"

He blinked, and their driver glanced back toward them. "No. I was raised in a creche, educated as a Nool, was given a position at a variety of establishments, and completed my evolution into a Regiz six years ago."

She blinked. "I never think of the Nool as becoming something else."

"We all started that way. There are only three branches of the Rrassic that do not evolve from the Nool form. None of them are here. They are all high status."

She nodded. "So, do they ever occur in the population at large?"

"Only when the Sthik lay eggs. They are a one-in-five-thousand appearance."

"How many Rrassic is Saya?"

"One in three thousand. They are unexpected when they evolve, but they are welcome if they can remain sane."

"Is that a concern?"

"One in five is overwhelmed by the minds around them, but there is no one better for watching the overall health of a colony if they manage to make it through their training."

Niiva sighed. "That sucks."

"It does indeed. Ah, here we are."

The vehicle paused at three checkpoints, and they had to produce their identification at each one.

The gestation centre looked like an average medical centre if you didn't notice all the protection that surrounded it.

She whispered, "So, if a Saya has a child, does it have a higher chance of being a Saya?"

Argo shrugged. "Saya tend to remain alone, so I don't believe it has ever been tested."

"That's sad. Every other kind of Rrassic can seek companionship. Why not the Saya?"

"Saya can read the minds of anyone near them. That is not a comfortable thing for most."

Niiva frowned. "Nor for the Saya. That would suck."

"Apparently, it is why they prefer solitude. The Saya who works with the overseer is the only one allowed a dwelling outside the city."

Niiva's attention was fixed on the building. "What is the fail rate of the canisters?"

"Gestation, in general, can have a success rate as low as five percent with certain species blends. With humans, there will be a five to ten percent rejection rating at the most. We are a very close match."

"Now that alterations to the humans have been made."

He sighed. "Yes, that as well."

Their vehicle came to a halt, and the driver got out to release them from the car. They had been held captive in the back during the ride and would be searched on the way out. The Rrassic took their new offspring seriously, and no one was going to have a chance to steal them away to a wild colony world.

Niiva had learned about the wild colonies the night before while lying in Argo's arms, and she thought about them as she noted all the security in place for the protection of the next generation. Humans had been stolen and taken off world. This was one of the reasons that peacekeepers were essential. If a human saw something, she needed to feel safe in calling for help.

They checked in at the desk and were assigned a medic for their tour.

"In the future, you need only check in at the desk, and you will be able to go and visit your offspring whenever you like."

The medic was a Zjin-Rrassic. His stripes and heavily muscled shoulders looked a little out of place in the blue medic uniform. Niiva was used to the unrelieved black that the Rrassic wore.

"How quickly will the cells develop?" She was not able to imagine them as children.

"Five months from now the decanting will occur. You will be called for the event, and you can decide if you want to raise your children for a few years or to put them in a creche. Both options are available." The medic smiled kindly.

Argo put his arm around her. "We will discuss it."

Niiva was holding her breath as they took a secured lift to the floor where the canisters were installed.

It looked like a library waiting for books. There was one shelf that was occupied, and Niiva walked straight for it.

There was a set of three canisters nestled together, and

they all had little silvery babies halfway through development. Another canister a few spaces away had a slightly smaller developing creature, but the fifth visibly occupied canister had a nearly fully developed baby in it. The child had slightly pointed ears, and its sex couldn't be determined from the angle it was lying in, but it looked nearly ready to be born.

"Wow. It's huge."

The medic chuckled. "We were lucky that an accelerator was found among your people. We hope that she is receptive again soon, but time will tell."

On a shelf to her right were two glowing canisters, and she smiled at the miniscule specks that were floating around in them.

"My tiny contributions to the world. Oh, and Argo's, of course." She smiled at him. She leaned forward to look, but the medic put his hand on her shoulder.

He walked to the edge of the shelf, and with a smooth motion, he pulled out a lens. With an easy stride, he moved back to her and arranged the lens in front of the first canister.

"Oh, wow. It is a little cluster. A teeny ball." She felt Argo next to her, and she moved over so he could look.

To her astonishment, he blinked rapidly to clear his vision. Smiling, she took his hand and squeezed it.

She looked at the medic. "What are the options for viability? The likelihood of survival."

"The cellular replication is energetic and proceeding according to our estimates. They are both girls, by the way."

Argo swayed.

She held him and moved the lens over to the next canister. "Look, she has your eyes."

The medic snorted, and Argo narrowed his eyes at her.

"Not funny."

"No, but they are cells right now, and I have helped to inseminate enough cows to know that not every start has a happy ending. When they are past the sixty percent development mark, I will be more impressed. For now, I just can't get myself involved for fear of what is likely to happen."

Argo put his arms around her. "We are better at taking care of our developing population than cows are. I was grown in a canister like this from cells donated by one of our breeding queens, as were all of the Rrassic here. The egg supply has run out, so now, we are trying to work through this in the most direct way possible. The women who can breed with us will supply the population for the next generation."

She sighed against him and inhaled his sunny and spicy scent. "What about those who can't?"

"They will still help by assisting us with supporting the next generation."

"Well, that is something, I guess." She muttered it against his chest. "When I figured out what I was, I never expected this."

"Everyone here was grown in a canister, just as our children will be. With the alterations to our physiology, it would be dangerous for you to attempt a standard pregnancy."

"You don't get it. I never thought I would be able to have children. I mean, why else have clones?"

He chuckled, and he stroked her hair. "The term Breeders didn't tip you off?"

"I thought that was just about sex."

He chuckled. "That is a very important part of it. The men here were chosen because their features matched what the majority of humans consider to be attractive. Other species have different interests, so on other worlds, the Rrassic have a different appearance."

The medic cleared his throat. "Is she authorized for that

information?"

Argo spoke over her head. "She is aware of the origin of her kind on Imrahl. She got the information on her own."

The medic made a small noise. "Has she informed anyone?"

Niiva spoke against Argo's chest. "She has not. It would not help her people to have this concern on their shoulders and would destabilize many. I don't want to hurt any of the women here."

The medic sighed and nodded. "Well, your two daughters are healthy for now. Feel free to come back at any time to visit them."

Niiva looked back at the tiny blobs under the magnification of the lens. "I will think about."

The medic walked away, and Niiva went to look at the little blobs. "What do you want to name them?"

Argo chuckled and wrapped his arms around her again. "What do you want to name them?"

"Abigail and Teeree." She wrinkled her nose and stroked the canisters in turn.

"Good names. Once decanted, they will be Abigail and Teeree Niiva-Argo."

She chuckled. "Niiva-Argo?"

"If you choose another mate, his name will come last on his offspring."

"Right. So, it is a built-in genetic tracking."

"Correct."

She leaned her head against him. "Do you think I am going to seek out another mate?"

"We do not know much about each other yet. That seems to be an important side of human mating practices."

Niiva nodded. "True, but some of us go on instinct, as flawed as it is."

"I have enjoyed your instinct."

She chuckled. "I have enjoyed yours as well, but I still don't know why you tracked me down."

He chuckled and squeezed her. "Because you faced off against two Regiz with nothing to defend yourself but the helmet."

"Interesting. So, my attitude attracted you? I thought all the Regiz were obsessed with appearance."

"We are, but some of us are aberrant and actually seek out females with aggressive tendencies."

"Perverts."

He leaned down and nipped her ear. "You appeared to enjoy it."

"It seems so long ago. I think you need to refresh my memory." She turned in his arms and looked up through her lashes.

His mood went from teasing to tense in a second. The vein in his neck pulsed under the gold of his hide.

"I believe we should get back to your quarters."

She smiled. "I thought that shopping was also on the agenda."

He sighed, and it was a rough sound. "Right. Will you promise not to be suggestive while we choose your new wardrobe?"

"I will try. I probably won't succeed, but I will try."

He leaned down and pressed his forehead to hers. "Try hard."

She blinked, and her body warmed. "Now, who is being suggestive?"

His smile at the close range showed a lot more fang than she remembered him having. Her memory went back to the feel of those teeth in her neck, and her good intentions wavered.

"Right. Go, shop, home." She pushed at him, and he chuckled, leading the way out of the library because she couldn't think of anything else to call it in her mind.

"Yes, pet."

She was going to have to get him to stop calling her that, but keeping her breathing even and her pulse normal was her primary focus. Her muscles were still sore, but she had a very good idea of what to do to loosen them up.

Horizontal therapy was something to look forward to.

Chapter Eight

The shopping took an hour, and there were quite a few Rrassic who came by the shop door to watch her trying on clothing. Some of those guys had a fetish that needed attending to.

The sports tops were her favourite acquisition. She was delighted with the supply she had gotten and a little surprised that she was being issued with a peacekeeper uniform before she had finished her training.

They were back in the secured vehicle and on their way to the Breeder compound when she asked, "Why the gowns?"

Argo shrugged. "If you want to go to any of the social events, you might want to wear a gown. There are socials and dances nearly every night of the week, and it is an excellent way to socialize with the other Breeders as well as any that you might prefer as a match."

She tensed her lips. "Stop offering me other males. It makes me want to hesitate instead of crawling into your lap until we are both exhausted."

The driver glanced back at her, and she smiled slightly.

He exhaled slowly and continued until they were going through the initial security gate. It seemed he had to focus the entire way.

Niiva smiled at him as she left the vehicle, and Argo carefully bustled her into the complex. They registered in, and then, they walked to the stairs that would take them up to her floor. A gathering of women was in the atrium, and there was a lot of giggling.

"What is going on there?"

Argo glanced back and kept walking. "They are teaching the ins and out of sex with the Rrassic."

Niiva chuckled. "There is certainly a lot of that if you do it right."

He growled, and she sprinted up the steps, fighting the muscles in her legs that told her she was done for the day.

Staggering to her door, she opened it with the signal from the wrist band that she and all the other humans had gotten when they were assigned to their workplaces.

She grunted as she walked into her apartment, and she glanced back to see Argo closing and latching the manual lock on her door.

Niiva waited. "What is on the agenda tomorrow?"

"More combat practice and you might get to beat up the simulator." He moved toward her with a slow and deliberate step.

Niiva blinked. He was stalking her. She decided to derail him a little. She kicked off her shoes and loosened the closure of her trousers, letting them drop to the floor.

He froze in place.

She grinned and lifted her tunic over her head, dropping it to the ground before she skimmed out of her panties and then her bra. "Sir, I believe that I have plans for you, and it involves you seated comfortably so I can have my way with you. Nudity is preferable."

His tunic hit her in the face, and by the time she clawed it away, he was pulling the last tube of fabric from his leg. He was gold from head to toe, and his erection was flared with a slick head.

She grinned and beckoned to him, walking back into the living room and pointing to the couch. "Sit."

He reached for her, and she stepped back. "Sit."

His frown should have been unattractive, but she wanted

to stroke his brow and nibble at his lower lip.

When he was seated, she walked toward him and kissed his lips. He threaded his hand into her hair, so the duelling of his tongue with hers was enough to make her pulse thump in her groin.

She braced one hand on his shoulder, and the other reached between his thighs to stroke him slowly. He shuddered, and she felt more of his teeth and a slight prick on the inside of her lip. She pulled back and looked into his eyes. "So, this time, I am in charge. Next time, you can have your turn again."

He grinned. "Excellent."

She knew she was wet and she would have no difficulty getting him inside her. Holding off her own orgasm would be the difficult part. She was nearly cumming, and all she had was an alien warrior at her mercy.

She slowly straddled his hips and set her knees next to his hips, reaching between their bodies and moving his cock into contact with her wet folds.

He shuddered. "Do you know what you are doing?"

She shook her head. "Nope. This is an experiment, but if it works, I would like to do it again."

She felt the tip of him slip inside her, and she looked up to meet his gaze as she lowered herself slowly and deliberately until the width of his slightly tapering penis got stuck. She gripped his shoulders and slowly pulled herself up again, and a deep and ragged sigh went through her at the delicious sensation.

"Let me help."

She looked at him, and he slid his hands under her shaking thighs. She smiled. "Thank you. Today might not have been the best day for this."

He chuckled. "Let me be the judge of that."

He slowly lowered her, and she closed her eyes at the

blissful feeling of fullness. A sharp exhalation as he lifted her again and a slight mewl of disappointment escaped her throat. She frowned. "One day I am going to have you pinned under me."

"Today is not that day, but I do look forward to it." He grinned and lowered her on his cock once again.

She whimpered, and he repeated the motion, lifting and dropping her with a steady rhythm until she dug her nails in his shoulders. Her hoarse scream when her body bucked and clutched at him was swallowed by his mouth. He held her in place and shuddered as his hips bucked upward in short bursts.

When they unlocked from each other, she dropped her head to his shoulder. "That was fun, but I sort of . . ."

"What?" He ran a hand down her sweaty back.

"I sort of missed the bite."

"It will happen again when you are receptive."

"So, ovulating."

"Or just on the edge of it. Some of the other variants of Rrassic have specific methods for spurring ovulation. I have to wait until you are ready."

She chuckled and burrowed into his arms with his cock still throbbing inside her. "It looks like we have a tense month of waiting."

"Well, there are many things that we can try that would be easier if we weren't trying to get into a position where I can bite you."

She laughed. "You have plans?"

"Fantasies that spring to life whenever you touch me."

"That isn't all that springs to life." She did a slow stirring circle with her hips.

"Ah, yes. I am glad that the uniform contains a tailored tunic." There was a distinct amusement in his tone.

She sighed and simply held him, breathing in the scent of

sex. "Why did you take some of my blood?"

He chuckled. "You caught that?"

"I did."

"I was keying myself to you." He stroked his hands up and down her back.

"Why?"

"So that even if you are urged to mate with another male, I will remain faithful."

She blinked and looked up at him with a scowl. "The contract that was read out to us said that they couldn't force us to take multiple mates."

"They can't, but it might be requested of you regardless. I am keeping myself on standby for you at all times."

"That is very well and good, but it isn't going to happen. The more I learn about you, the more I like you."

She accepted his kiss, but she was still perturbed that he would think she would move on to another man.

He lifted his mouth from hers. "I am more than willing to father as many of your children as I can, but they are trying to draw the line at twenty children per breeding pair. We might reach that limit within the year if your cycle matches your scent."

"What does that mean?"

"You smell like you are approaching heat again, but it has only been a day since the last extraction. Your hormone levels should not be this high."

She pressed her forehead to his chest. "They shouldn't have selected me. This isn't a problem I want to pass to my daughters."

"Knowing what the issue is, gene therapies can be applied while the girls develop. Did you know that you have abnormal muscle, ligament, and bone development?"

"Uh, no. I didn't."

"Your children will be stronger and more durable than

the standard human-Rrassic hybrid."

She rubbed her cheek against his chest, enjoying the sensation. "Really? That's a good thing."

"Yes. It will take a few weeks to determine the effects of our particular blend of genes, but once we find out how many offspring we are allowed, we can make plans for the future."

She sighed and relaxed in his arms.

It took a few minutes, and he chuckled. "You are locked up, aren't you?"

She snorted. "Yes. Could you help me to the massage unit?"

"I will help you." He eased to the edge of the couch, and with his hands on her hips, he leaned forward and stood up.

Her head spun a little as he walked her into the bedroom and he continued to casually wear her as he lowered the massage bench before settling her on it and withdrawing his cock from inside her.

She blushed at the rush of fluid that left her, and her body bemoaned the heat that she had been stealing from him.

He winked and left her for a moment, returning with wraps that he placed over her and under her. She blinked when she was lifted out of the way, but the fabric was warm and snuggly. He eased her limbs straight and smiled. "Now, I am going to give you a rub down and try to work out some of the strain you put on yourself earlier today."

"The machine can do it."

"The machine can't find the joints and ligaments that you used because it wasn't watching."

He left and returned from the bathroom with a bottle of oil. The wrap on her was warming, and she looked down at it. "Why is this wrap warm?"

"It is designed for this purpose. Believe it or not, Rrassic need rubdowns as well. The heat helps our muscles, just like it does yours."

She nodded, and he folded the wrap up to her waist then he rubbed his hands with the oil. He slicked her up and then began to do long pulls on the front of her thighs.

She grunted as the muscle groups were worked on over the next hour and a half. Niiva had never had a massage so thorough, nor one that had given as much attention to her ass. He had begun on her butt when she flipped over, and he kept returning to it and the curve between waist and hip.

She was exhausted and sweaty, but she asked, "Are you just taking care of your favourite parts?"

He chuckled. "Your figure sends my senses reeling. I love the feel of your hips and the resilience of your flesh under my hands."

She was going to be bruised from the massage. That much she was aware of. There was no way that the pummelling she had gotten wouldn't leave a mark, and the massage had been thorough as well.

Chapter Nine

It took all week, but she finally began to make progress on the simulator. It had stopped dying, so that was definitely a good thing.

Niiva stood over the simulation of a Zjin-Rrassic, and it was on the ground, unconscious.

"Match to Niiva. No fatalities." The computer spoke calmly.

Argo rushed up to her and hugged her. "Well done, Niiva!"

She sighed and removed the wraps from her hands behind his back. "Session concluded."

The solid projection of the Rrassic opponent was removed.

Applause started from around the edges of the workout arena.

She glanced at the men who had watched her learn how to fight in Rrassic style, and then, she looked up at her mate. "I am very glad that I got the hang of this. I was tired of smashing them."

He kissed her in front of the watchers without concern. "I know, pet. On the plus side, you have two days off coming."

She grinned. "I know. Do you?"

He chuckled. "I do. So, what would you like to do?"

A cleared throat near them made her turn her head. Lianne and Sorrok were standing together.

"If you have finished dispatching your opponent, I need to continue my training. I envy you your strength. I just have chronic irritation on my side." Lianne winked.

Sorrok chuckled. "She really does. It is amazing. It can flare up at any time and burn for hours."

Lianne elbowed him in the ribs.

"See?" Sorrok's grin belied his aggrieved tone.

Lianne sighed. "Come on." She stalked onto the mat with her hands wrapped and her posture indicating that she was in the mood to fight someone.

Sorrok grinned and went to fight with his mate. Lianne was still working toward subduing her mate.

Argo kept his arm around her and walked her back to the changing area. "The computer is registering your capability; now, you need to work on your knowledge of laws governing Imrahl."

She groaned. "There are so many."

"I know, and I can't help you with this. You have passed the physical requirements of the peacekeeper position. Now, you have to work on the legal portion. I have confidence in your intelligence."

She exhaled sharply and stalked into the ladies' change area. Education was not her strength. She had gotten through life being enthusiastic and buxom. She wasn't unintelligent, but learning didn't come easily.

This was a mountain of work, and she was going to have to find a way to work around her normal thought patterns.

Niiva was excited. She had never been to one of the concerts in the park before.

Argo was carrying a basket in the hand that wasn't holding hers, and he was shaking his head. "I can't believe that you haven't been to one of these events before."

"I was busy or asleep in my quarters." She shrugged and looked around at the groups of women gathered on the greens. There were about three hundred women out on their day off, six hundred Rrassic were waiting, and when the ladies picked their spots, the Rrassic moved to settle in between them.

She giggled. "Wow. They are really persistent."

He walked her to an open spot near a tree and flicked open the blanket. "They need to be. You know what is at stake."

She rubbed the bridge of her nose. "Yes, I read up on Rrassic history last night, as you know. Lianne said that Sorrok showed her vids."

"I bet he did," Argo growled, and he set their picnic to one side while he sat and held his hand out to her. "Come on."

She was wearing one of her new outfits, and while it wasn't a ballgown, it was a pair of boots and a wrap dress. It exaggerated her figure ridiculously, but Argo stopped talking whenever he saw it. She made sure she wasn't going to get it dirty before she crouched and settled against her chosen mate.

He leaned back against the tree, and she settled against him, kissing him occasionally when he leaned toward her.

Some of the humans in their area were glaring at her, and she simply smiled and ran her hand down Argo's thigh. Their blush and averted eyes were enough of a result.

"Don't tease them, Niiva."

She chuckled. "I am just giving their minds another path to follow."

He sighed. "Fine, then don't tease me."

She looked down, and her hand was so far up his thigh she could feel the ridge of his erection. "Oops. Sorry."

She got up and shifted her position to sit across his thighs. "There. Better?"

He wrapped one arm around her hip and slid the other into the fold of her dress until he touched skin. "Much."

The concert began, and the alien songstresses sent their voices soaring through the crowd and wrapping around their minds.

Niiva watched as the gathered folk looked at the stage with hypnotic fascination. "What the heck? It sounds nice, but it isn't something I would fixate on."

Argo lowered his head until his lips were against her ear, and he explained the purpose of the concerts.

Limura singers activated the libido in both humans and Rrassic. The concerts were designed to get more physical interaction between the two species.

She whispered for his ears only. "So, why isn't it working on me?"

His hand moved under her dress, and he cupped her breast. "Isn't it?"

She chuckled. "It really isn't."

"Ah, you are always in that state. There is no repression to work with."

She nodded and leaned up to kiss him as the songs swirled out and left her behind. Ah well, they were still lovely to listen to.

Niiva cuddled with Argo while the attendants of the concert filed out. They had finished their picnic during intermission, but sitting in his lap had been the best seat in the house, so she was still on his lap when they found themselves nearly alone.

Niiva smiled and got to her feet, freeing Argo. She watched him bend over and admired the view.

When he had tidied it all up and they turned to leave, a group of a half-dozen Rrassic moved to block their way. There was a girl with a dazed expression being held up between a Luthin and Zjin-Rrassic, and that looked suspicious. The Luthin didn't tend to go for group scenes.

Niiva blinked, and Argo moved to her side.

One of the Regiz called out. "You are not taking care of your mate, brother. I can smell her heat from here."

Niiva frowned. "Rude."

Argo spoke softly. "As you stated, she is my mate. You have no say in what we do or don't do."

Niiva looked at the men and took in their stance, their mixed grouping, and finally, she looked for their ident bands. She glanced at Argo. He nodded slightly. He had seen what she had.

Argo followed up with, "Just as I have no say over what she does."

With that sentence, she knew he was encouraging her to do whatever it took.

She took a few steps toward the men. "Why are her pupils dilated, and why are you holding her up?"

"Why do you have the aura of a woman in heat?" The Regiz moved toward her.

Two of the men were moving toward Argo, and two were backing up the friend that was coming for her.

"Oh, that? That is natural. It is just part of the joy of being me."

She felt the air change behind her. A Luthin must be ambushing her. She pulled out a memory of a bar fight and focused on getting out of this in one piece, her mate alive, with the lady who had definitely been drugged.

Niiva might not be a peacekeeper yet, but there was no time like the present to practice.

Time slowed, and hands grabbed her from behind, lifting her off her feet. The Regiz in front of her flicked out a hypo, and that was not something that Niiva was interested in.

She kicked back at the Luthin with all her strength and felt his knee go sideways. The wet popping sound came after the impact.

He dropped, and she ducked under the arm of the Regiz, snapping her hand upward. She pulled her hit enough that she was pretty sure she hadn't broken his neck.

The two men behind him grabbed at her while their companion dropped. They were two feet away from her when there was a rush of Hunters from every shadow.

Argo yelled out, "Niiva, hold. Don't hurt them."

She backed away from the men and ran to intercept the two who were escaping with their prisoner. They stuffed her into a small vehicle and took off.

Grabbing one of the cycles that appeared to have been waiting for one of the kidnappers, she fired it up and took off after the vehicle, not letting it out of her view.

She shot past them and cut them off, dropping the cycle in front of their vehicle before jumping to safety.

The vehicle struck the cycle and careened into a storefront. Niiva approached the vehicle, and hands grabbed her again. A hypo hissed against her neck, and she went down.

Argo clutched his side and moved to follow his mate. They were going to try and get her off world if they could subdue her.

"Go to medical, Argo. We have already shut down the portal. Your mate won't be taken anywhere." Heronik helped him to his feet.

"No, you don't understand what she is. I have to get to her."

Heronik caught him. "She will be fine. The men were right on her tail."

"This feels wrong. I have to go after her." He got up and staggered.

Heronik sighed. "Fine. Guys, a little help."

Argo felt his side burn as he was supported to a vehicle,

and they followed the path that Niiva had taken.

The ditched cycle was twisted and warped, but the vehicle in the building showed them why.

"See? No one got away."

The human woman inside the vehicle groaned and clutched her head. The Zjin at her side was bleeding badly, and the Luthin driver appeared to have not survived the crash.

The woman called out. "I need to get out of here. She's still nearby, but she can't talk."

Argo grunted and staggered out of the vehicle. "You saw her?"

"No, but she is here. She is close. She needs help."

He nodded and saw the far-off look in her eyes. He had seen that once before, and while he didn't think humans had Trackers, he wasn't about to argue. "Where? Show me."

The other Hunters argued with him, but he walked with the swaying woman, and she took him down an alley with six men in tow.

The edge of Niiva's boot was behind a stack of boxes. The woman went quiet, and she pointed.

There was a rush as the Hunters followed the silent command, and when the Luthin was subdued, one of the Regiz carried an unconscious Niiva out from the spot behind the boxes. Argo's knees buckled.

"Is she all right?"

"She is. She has been given a paralytic."

The woman next to Argo nodded. "That is why I could hear her. She was screaming."

Heronik cleared his throat. "You were right; now, let's get your knowledgeable ass over to the medical centre. You are bleeding out."

Argo watched his mate carried off and surrendered to his friend and the other Hunters' assistance. The human woman was walking with one of the others, and Argo was content to have Niiva near him as they were transported to the med centre so she could wake up and he could make it through the night.

This was not a proper first date from what he had learned about human mating behaviours, but Niiva did seem to do her own thing with alarming regularity.

He had better work on his own combat training if he was going to keep up with his mate.

Chapter Ten

Niiva came out of the sedation with a gasp. She bolted upright, but the medic next to her held her to the bed.

"Stay still, Peacekeeper Niiva. The medication they gave you was a little unusual."

The woman at the side of the bed was familiar. "He isn't kidding. That shit was nasty."

Niiva looked over at her, and she blinked. "You were the one that they were holding."

"Yeah. I was also the one in the car you crashed. Nice work, by the way." The woman touched the bruise on her forehead.

"Can't they fix that?" Niiva eased herself to a sitting position, pausing as her head spun.

The medic muttered and gave her a hypo that helped her head clear slightly. "But stay in bed. When your mate has finished his treatment, I will send him in."

She went cold. "Treatment?"

"Yes, he was injured in the sting operation yesterday." The medic offered the information casually.

"Wait, it was a sting?"

She was seething, and the woman next to her reached out and patted her hand. "Calm down, Niiva. You are cursing really loudly."

"I didn't say anything."

The woman smiled. "I know. Seriously. Argo is fine. I can feel him through your connection. He is irritated and worried about you and also worried that you are going to start looking for another mate with one of the guys here in the med centre."

"How do you know all this?"

The woman smiled and shrugged. "I have no idea. My brain just came online two days ago. One day I was working at a delivery service, and the next, I was hearing thoughts at close range."

"You are kidding."

"I wish I was. It really sucks." The woman smirked and then blinked. "Oh, right. Sorry. I am Sarah Wilkerson."

Niiva was taken aback. She had been wondering who the woman was, and now, she had the answer.

"Argo is on his way here, so I should leave you two alone." Sarah got to her feet with a smile.

"Wait, are you going to the Breeders compound?"

Sarah shrugged. "I don't know. I am not receptive, I am just telepathic. They are going to have to find somewhere to keep me."

Niiva's eyes widened. "How much of my mind did you read?"

"Oh, I knew that part already. I walked past the overseer and his mate, and she was concerned about more of the humans waking to the realization. I am cool with it, and it does explain the change from the mild empathy that I remember to this." She tapped her forehead.

Sarah winked. "I will see you later. I am fairly sure of it."

"Thank you, it was nice to wake up to a familiar face, Sarah."

"It wasn't a problem. You were so concerned about my survival that I thought you should see that your actions had a positive result. I will see you soon, Peacekeeper Niiva. I am sure of it."

Sarah left the room, and through the frosted wall, Niiva saw two guards take up position on either side of her while two more positioned themselves outside Niiva's room.

Niiva waited, and in twenty heartbeats, Argo walked in. He looked drawn and pale under his golden hide, but aside from the bloody gash on his side, he looked fine.

Niiva extended her hand out to him, and he walked to her, bowing carefully, turning her hand over and placing a kiss in her palm. "You are awake."

The medic at her side sighed. "And she is refusing the bedrest that she needs. Her physiology did not agree with that paralytic. She will be dizzy and lightheaded for a few days."

"How long do you need her here?" Argo was serious.

The medic looked at him. "At least overnight."

"Is there a larger bed?"

Niiva caught on and turned to her side, scooting to one edge of the bed that had been sized for a prone Rrassic. "Hop on carefully, Argo."

The bed moved slightly, and her mate wrapped himself around her.

"Were you badly injured?" She pulled his arm around her waist and held his hand.

He murmured, "My wound would not have widened if I hadn't gone to find my mate. As it was, I am glad I did. No one else was going to do it."

"Did you meet Sarah?"

"The woman in the car? Yes. She tracked you."

"She's a telepath."

"I did get that impression." He nuzzled her ear.

The medic finished his fussing and took one final scan before he wheeled the kit out of the room.

Niiva yawned. "Are you sure you are all right?"

"I will heal. I am glad that he didn't take you anywhere."

"Why didn't he?"

Argo cleared his throat. "Because you were always meant to be a target. You are a fantastic specimen, and the colonists are all over your genetic pattern. They want women like you, even more than we do. You are a glowing jewel of genetic triumph."

"Cut the manure. What was going on?"

"To get you off world they needed a portal. Because we knew their target, we just had to watch for the power surge of an opening portal. They sent the Hunters there to close the portal and arrest the colonists, and then, we faced off against the remainder in the park. The men had no idea we had closed the portal, and their taking of Sarah made things awkward."

"You used me as bait."

"The overseer used you as bait. I figured things out when they suggested that I take you to the concert."

"You could have told me."

"I was having too nice a time." He rubbed his chin against her head.

She chuckled. "I am going to make you pay for that."

"I don't mind. Now, rest and recover. I want you back to your feisty self tomorrow."

"Nothing like a deadline to health." She inhaled deeply and then exhaled slowly. Argo's arm was around her, and they cuddled together on the med bed.

She could kick his butt for not warning her later, for now, she was just glad that he was alive and safe. Niiva had the feeling that they had come very close to losing each other, and it was not a great sensation. She could be outraged when her heart wasn't aching over the near miss.

Having breakfast in the overseer's boardroom was not the way that Niiva had planned her day. Mind you, she hadn't thought of much beyond another nap in her own bed with Argo next to her.

Argo was holding her hand, but the gathering of other

Rrassic and their mates was a little odd for first thing in the morning. In the corner was the Saya, but he wasn't speaking, he was observing.

Iktabi cleared his throat. "So, last evening, there was another attempt to gain humans for the colonists. The attempt was foiled due to a psychic leak."

Niiva nodded with a grimace.

Iktabi inclined his head. "I apologize for using you as bait, Niiva, but you are by far the most noticeable of the new Breeders."

"I grudgingly accept your apology, but if it happens again, let me know so that I can arm myself or, at least, have an antidote for that drug." Niiva blinked. "I am still shaking it off."

She felt a cool touch on her mind and looked over to Lehkor. He was giving her a quick mental assessment.

Argo squeezed her hand. "You are fine."

"You got sliced open and then nearly bled out chasing me."

The others around the table looked concerned.

Iktabi got their attention again. "It was regrettable, but we now have several of the colonists to interrogate as to the whereabouts of their worlds and what kind of step-down or step-up protocols are needed."

Bree leaned forward. "Are the babies in danger?"

Iktabi shook his head. "No. We have high security on the gestation centre. That is the one place I am not worried about. Our protocols have been stepped up since your canister was added. That is a child worth stealing."

Bree exhaled and clutched her mate's hand. "What do we do when she is out?"

"That is what we are here for. Our intent was for you and your mates to remain with the population at the Breeder compound, but now, it is becoming clear that the humans on

Imrahl are developing secondary talents."

Lianne frowned as did Bree.

Isabella smiled and explained, "Because of the food, the environment, and the stimuli, things become apparent that weren't apparent before. Lianne, you became more aggressive. Bree, your genes kicked into high gear when you mated with Arix, and your children will continue to develop at double the standard rate."

Niiva nodded. "I got stronger. Much, much stronger."

Isabella continued. "And I got access to a lot of information, which makes me a security risk. A Saya could peel me open in seconds."

Niiva nodded, unsure if she was supposed to mention Sarah.

"Do not mention Sarah. She is under guard until I can assist her in closing her mind at will."

She didn't stare at Lekorh, but she wanted to.

Bree cleared her throat. "Right. So, as we all have children in the gestation centre, this is the best time to ask where do we want them raised?"

Niiva blinked and asked, "Is it okay if I don't want to raise my own?"

Two out of the three women looked shocked, but Isabella smiled. "It is fine. I have done extensive research on the creche system that the Rrassic have in place, and you would be able to communicate with your children without raising them. They will be made to understand the situation."

Bree frowned. "What if I want to raise my child?"

Lianne nodded. "Me too."

Their Rrassic looked to Iktabi. He smiled. "I was hoping that you would decide that. It will get to the heart of what I am about to say."

Everyone was paying attention.

Iktabi looked around. "Most of you are aware that Imrahl is a world accessed through portals, but what the Rrassic have done is to create dozens of worlds that are out of step with this one, worlds where we can raise and train our next generation. We have created worlds where time marches quickly, so if you go to raise your child, years will pass for you but only weeks will pass here."

Lianne nodded. "It is how you have Rrassic that are compatible with our race, right? You built them."

Iktabi nodded. "And others built me. I grew up in a pocket dimension, just as your mates did. The Voboth, or Yoboth, if you prefer, are not kind, do not care for beings that walk instead of glide, and outnumber the Rrassic vastly. In order to gain our numbers, we had to use all the tools at our disposal. Hiding in pockets where time moves more quickly or slowly is our weapon in this war."

Niiva cocked her head. "Will they come back here as Nools?"

Iktabi smiled. "They will complete their training with their families, but they will come back as warriors. Do not doubt that. They are our key to survival."

Arix asked, "What if we have another child while we are at the creche?"

"Medical facilities will be available to you. Your children will be safe, and you can continue your reproduction."

Arix sighed in relief and squeezed Bree's hand. He looked over to Niiva, and he grinned with pride. "Our daughter will be decanted this week. The first human-Rrassic child."

Niiva bit her lip and said, "Well done, Bree and Arix. Bree, I bet you never saw him coming."

Bree paused, and then, she burst into giggles.

Arix flickered slightly as he fought the urge to go invisible when he caught onto the joke.

Chuckles ran through the meeting, and they determined that Bree and Arix would go first, followed by Lianne and Sorrok when their children were ready for decanting.

Volunteers would be taken from the other pairings that were currently trying to get a set of embryos of their own.

Iktabi followed up with, "Bree and Arix, if you reach your maximum offspring, please take steps to freeze any additional embryos."

Bree wrinkled her nose. "Twenty seems like a lot."

Lianne nodded. "Unless you have multiples; then, it will be over with you very quickly."

Bree nodded. "Fair point. Right. I am going to pack. I just have one question."

Iktabi smiled and raised his brows. "Yes?"

"Is there a beach? I do long for a beach."

He chuckled. "There is a beach. It is an island city with the portal above a very deep ocean. If you don't have a reception waiting for you or if you don't come through with a flying transport, I hope that you can swim."

The ladies looked at each other and smiled. Niiva imagined Argo lying out in the sun and relaxing, all of his muscle groups gleaming in the light and on display.

Argo cuddled her against him, and he stated, "I believe Niiva needs some rest."

Iktabi looked at him. "I need to speak with you two in the morning."

Niiva smiled blandly. "As long as it is in the morning, we will be here."

Isabella's shoulders were shaking, and the other ladies were grinning. The lust of the newly mated was something that was whispered about in the atrium of the Breeder compound.

The gossip was familiar, all they needed back at the compound was a stripper pole for dance practice, and it would feel like home.

Niiva said her goodbyes, and she and Argo headed off to the Breeder compound under guard.

"I am sorry that I didn't tell you about the operation."

She patted his thigh. "You got stabbed for it, so I think we learned from this experience."

He laughed the entire ride, and the smile on his face turned to bliss when she sprawled him on the bed and did all the work for a change.

Chapter Eleven

Niiva looked at her wardrobe and glanced back at Argo on the bed. "I thought you said that the uniform came today."

He grinned. "It did. It is to your left. Isabella did some of the design work on it so that it is more appropriate for you."

She frowned and pulled out what was a black dress at first glance. "Holy heck."

"I believe there are leggings in with it."

Niiva turned back to the bed and stalked over to him. "How do you know so much about it?"

He chuckled and rolled to his back, stretching luxuriously. "I don't sleep as much as you do, and Isabella wished for feedback on her designs. I am not an excellent arbiter when it comes to fashion, but the designs looked easy to move in. You are going to be the test case for the uniforms of the female peacekeepers."

Niiva scowled. "I am the guinea pig?"

"I am not precisely sure what that is, but I will say yes."

She grinned. "I haven't tested anything to destruction before. This is going to be fun."

Argo sat up. "You might want to contact Isabella to make sure that that is what she had in mind."

"I will." She sprinted to the com centre and dialled up Isabella's desk code.

Isabella's face came into view, and she blinked. "Uh, hello, Niiva."

"Hiya. There is a uniform in my size in my closet. Is there

a reason for it?"

"Oh, yes. You are to test it to check its durability and range of motion. The guys don't really design around breasts that much. They don't know what they do in combat situations."

Niiva laughed.

"Speaking of which, what size are you, double D?"

Niiva looked down and then she jerked the fabric of the uniform over her chest. "Sorry."

"Not a problem. I have seen a lot more. Well, not more but additional nudity." Isabella grinned. "When you have finished working out in the uniform, send it back to our office with any notes you care to add."

"Excellent. I will get to it."

"Good. I expect tattered clothing in our office by the end of the day." She winked and closed the call.

Niiva looked at the fabric that was covering her. "My friend, you have met your match."

She got up and returned to the bedroom. "Okay. I have free rein to destroy this if it is necessary."

"So, shall we head to the gym?"

"I think that is a splendid idea."

She got dressed in the uniform and did a few squats. The skirt was too long. She would trip on it. The shoulders were too tight, and her boobs were going to pop out if she reached up over her head.

"This is fascinating to watch."

She gave him a dark look and reached down to touch her toes. "Keep staring. It is going to get weirder."

She pulled on boots that matched the uniform, and she turned side to side to look in the mirror. The suit was baggy at the waist and too tight on her hips. It looked fine until she moved; then, fabric bunched everywhere.

"This is bizarre. Your tailors are normally so accurate."

She frowned.

"Your body has different points of rotation. Your curves hold the fabric in a way that my body won't."

She did a few jumping jacks and sighed. The fabric wasn't going to break, but it didn't play nicely either.

"Right. Let's go." She finished gawking at herself and looked at Argo. He could get dressed in a hurry, and she envied the ease and fit of his clothing right then.

They left her quarters, and she walked at his side. It wouldn't do to hang onto him with her uniform on.

The security officer that drove them to the gym made her frown. She asked Argo, "How is this going to work when I am actually employed as an officer? I can't run around with a bodyguard."

"It will be worked out. This peacekeeper setup is Isabella's brainchild, or so Iktabi has said."

"Wow, you really get a lot of inside information."

"Iktabi has been a source of calm and reason while I have been trying to figure out this situation. The Rrassic dream of finding a mate, but few folks tell us what to do once we find them." He sighed, and the driver laughed.

She shook her head. "And men say that women gossip."

"Human men, maybe. Our Rrassic brethren are the only ones who understand what we are going through. We counsel each other the same way that you speak to the human women around you. They will come to you with questions, and you will use your experience with me and the others to fill in the parts of the dance that they are missing."

"The dance?"

"It is the only way we have to describe the courting of females from other species. We see what they will and will not tolerate and what they respond to."

"Wow. Okay. Sure. That makes a certain kind of sense."

The vehicle pulled up outside the gym, and she spoke to

the driver. "This isn't going to take long."

He grinned and nodded. He was a Nool with a cheerful demeanour, and she saw a sparkle in his black eyes.

She and Argo got out and entered the gym. Argo explained their purpose, and the Nool manning the counter nodded in amused understanding. Normally, no one brought in outside clothing.

The combat simulator was rough on her clothing, but it didn't tear. It did trip her, twist around her, and give her opponent handholds, and she and Argo got it all on the vid.

The recording was sent to the overseer's office. Niiva would send the clothing together with notes when she got back to the Breeder compound.

Argo was grinning when she leaned against him in the ride home.

"That was interesting. I have never seen anyone assaulted by their own clothing before."

She punched him lightly. "Is there a gym at the Breeder compound?"

"Yes, but it doesn't provide the audience that you need."

"I don't need an audience, I need the clothing to work with me, not against me."

He grinned. "I look forward to the evolution."

She grunted and tugged at the twisted fabric. "So do I."

He put his arm around her and held her during their drive back to the Breeder compound.

They were scanned through and taken to the front door of the complex.

The guard at the door grinned when he saw her. "You have a delivery, Niiva Dollard."

She blinked. "A what?"

"It was installed in the atrium. I confess as to a certain curiosity as to what you do with it."

Argo gave her a look and shrugged. "I didn't send it."

Curious herself, she wrestled with her clothing as she walked, stopping short when she saw the tall metallic pole on the wide platform. She stopped short. "Ohmygod."

Argo stared at it. "What is it?"

Several of the ladies were circling it and giggling, but no one made a move.

She wanted to cover her face, but instead, she held up a hand. "Does anyone have any music?"

Some of the authorized males from the bachelor quarters were gathering, but the women shooed them away.

Argo stood back, and she winked.

With a flourish, she unbuttoned the tunic and pulled it over her head, wearing the sports bra and tights with her boots.

She pushed at the pole, and it was delightfully sturdy. Niiva pulled herself up toward the top of the pole, and she looped her leg around it, spinning slowly as a song with a heavy beat thudded through the air.

She landed on her hands and flicked her legs free, standing straight and playing in a slow rotation before she spun and rocketed herself around the pole to the amusement of her fellow humans.

Bree was applauding with the others when the music stopped, and Niiva took a bow, laughing.

Bree grinned. "Were you a pro?"

"No, just an enthusiastic student. I liked to use my strength on something that I couldn't hurt."

She leaned down and scooped up her tunic. The ladies were clamouring for lessons.

"Let me get changed and we can arrange something. I am going to have to call the overseer's office to get a few more if I am going to teach a class though."

Argo blinked. "The overseer?"

She tapped the centre of her forehead. His eyes widened.

"Oh."

They headed up to her quarters, and she sighed. Technically, men didn't live in the Breeder quarters. They were the guests of the women, and that was all.

Once inside her quarters, she folded up the tunic, made some drawings on her tablet, and sent the file to Isabella, along with notes on why the current design was not acceptable.

She called up Isabella and smiled when the call was answered. "Right. I am sending you copies of the files with suggestions for things that I think will work a bit better."

"Like what?"

"One solid under layer with concealing and uniform components on top. A bodysuit with a vest and a skirt in place."

"Nice. I saw the vid from the gym. I can see most of the problems."

"Oh, and make sure that any skirt components end just below the knee. Hypo resistance would also be good as well as any kind of built-in body armour."

Isabella nodded. "First, we make it work, and then, we build in all the fancy bits."

"Works for me. Now, can you thank Lekorh for his gift and ask him if we can get a few more. The ladies want me to teach a class."

Isabella blinked. "What gift?"

"I muttered something in my mind, and he saw it. So, now, I am going to be teaching some of the ladies how to pole dance."

"Holy shit."

"Yeah, so for a class, I will need a few more poles."

"Of course. Can I be one of your students?" Isabella smiled. "I always wanted to take the classes but never had the time."

"I am not actually an instructor."

"You are the closest thing we have. I will tell Lekorh to triple whatever he ordered."

They exchanged a few more pleasantries, and then, Isabella went off to give orders to the only Saya-Rrassic on the planet. Well, everyone needed a hobby.

Chapter Twelve

She had a waiting list for classes that included every woman at the Breeder compound before she had even made it down the steps.

As Niiva spoke with them, she realized that not every woman had access to the gym or the combat simulators. The stripper pole was the closest to a workout that they could get unless they took an escort with them.

Bree spoke to her quietly. "I know. I thought they all had a mate as well, but they are just receptive, so if they choose a male, there is a chance of a pregnancy. If they don't choose, they are in a cycle of lockdown and evenings at the mixers."

Niiva winced. "Yikes. Even regular workers in the city can go to the gym."

"Not once they are found to be receptive. Their lives become a round of meeting men and dancing, as well as socializing here. They are going stagnant." Bree looked around at the women who were chattering excitedly about the new possibility in their midst.

Niiva looked at them and felt a sense of protectiveness rise in her chest. "Right. Well, it has only been a few months since women started to tick into the receptive category. I will find things for them to do."

Bree chuckled. "You are going to take them on?"

"I am. I am used to keeping my people busy, and I am just going to have to find safe outings and events for the ladies to attend while exposing them to the maximum amount of eligible Rrassic."

"You are going to take on the position of matchmaker?"

Niiva sighed. "More like an older sister. I am determined to fill the gestation library with children who aren't just mine."

Bree laughed. "Don't worry. We are just the first steps on what is going to become a very wild ride."

Niiva looked casually and saw Argo talking to some of the single Rrassic. "I have thought of myself as a wild ride a time or two, but this is a whole new level."

She chuckled. "I only just met you, but I am going to miss you when you go."

"I will be back before you know it. Possibly with a horde of children. My peculiarity is that I accelerate the gestation of any pregnancies I have. If I have a few more when I am out of here, I will be building my own blended army. I am hoping that they go Luthin when they are adults. I want Arix to see himself in them, or rather not, I guess." Bree chuckled.

Niiva smiled. "When my children are decanted, I am going to send them to your care."

Bree nodded. "And I will take excellent care of them. I have had to get used to the idea of being a mom. When Arix was sent off on a mission, I refused to let them take the child until he was there. It was a near thing. She almost killed me."

"Was it really that serious?"

"It was. There was no time for my body to adjust to what was going on inside it. I was being torn apart from the inside out."

Niiva blinked. "Damn."

"Yeah. How far along were you?"

She wrinkled her nose. "Less than three hours?"

Bree was amazed. "They could register it?"

"Apparently. For lack of a better term, I was in heat. My

scent indicates that I am nearly always in heat."

Bree winced. "That must be awkward."

"It is fine for me. I only have eyes for Argo. It is distracting for the unmated Rrassic though."

Bree laughed. "I imagine it would be."

Niiva shrugged. "It is fine."

She looked around. "Where is Lianne?"

"She is probably studying for the peacekeeper exam."

Niiva blinked. "Damn it. I am supposed to be doing that."

"Yes, but you have already passed the physical requirements. She hasn't. She has the technique but not enough stopping power."

Niiva nodded. "Right. Okay. So, I just need to catch up on the laws of Imrahl."

"It won't be too difficult. They mostly restrict the Rrassic behaviour when dealing with humans, and they control human behaviour after they have been confirmed receptive."

"You know a lot about this."

"I like to read. The regulations are an interesting read."

"Can you help me study? I have never been good at applied learning."

Bree looked around and saw Arix. She pointed at Niiva and upstairs.

He nodded and spoke to Argo. They both turned and nodded, so Bree and Niiva headed upstairs to her quarters.

Once inside the safe zone, Niiva brought up the files and then went to the kitchen and made tea, dispensing snacks from the unit in the corner.

Bree grinned. "You don't cook?"

"I do, but I haven't had a chance. This whole thing has spun me out of my comfort zone."

Bree chuckled. "Tell me about it. I was kidnapped, nearly killed, and then, I made a run for it on an alien world, only to be adopted by some very big and slobbery animals."

"But you were rescued."

"I was. Arix was sent to get me, and he was the first Rrassic that I ever felt anything for. The longer I was with him, the more I felt. Of course, he had to get used to my skark escort, but they accepted him, and I considered it a good sign. When we are together, it is just *right* somehow."

Niiva smiled. "I know that feeling. It is like they teach them patience or something. No matter how nuts I get, Argo just rolls with it."

"They are selected for temperament as well as appearance." Bree nodded as she poured tea.

"They would have to be." Niiva chuckled and carried the snacks while Bree brought the tea. They settled in the living space and looked at the monitor.

Bree asked her questions, and Niiva answered them, passing several hours in question and answer. Niiva knew more than she thought she did, but there were some finer points of behaviour that she needed to work on when it came to the law.

Rrassic men were actually authorized to push their seduction fairly far as long as the women weren't panicking. That was a bit appalling, but then, the women were clones of humans mixed with some Rrassic DNA. If a Rrassic woman were there, her responses would be obvious, and they would react accordingly. Social behaviours to keep men calm were acting against them when it came to making sure that the ladies were safe.

Niiva pinched her nose. "That is going to be a bit of a hard sell."

"Despite what you think, your pole dancing class should help. The ladies will get used to display in front of the guys, and they will have more of a connection between physical activity and pheromones."

Niiva sat back and drummed her fingers together. "I just

have to figure out how to educate them without seeming preachy."

"The dance of every teacher for time immemorial." Bree grinned.

"Yeah, I am also going to work with humans from different social situations around the world, and I will be speaking to them in a language not designed by humans. This won't be weird at all."

Bree cackled. "I wish I could be here when this was going on, but I think I will enjoy life with my little one, and possibly more of them."

"Is it weird that you will be a pocket of time?"

"No, the weirder thing is our increased life span. Once we have children, we are still going to have a few hundred years to kick around with our mates and hopefully grandchildren."

Niiva nearly keeled over. "Grandchildren."

"Of course. Our daughters will come back to Imrahl and find mates, possibly some of the men we turned down, or some of the Nool that have offered us medical assistance. This is what is happening, so all we can do is consume all the information we can and get ready for the next generation to come out of canisters, just like we did."

Niiva blinked. "What?"

"Don't worry if you knew and didn't mention it. Not many women would notice that their navel was slightly different, but I had a scar in mine that ended up gone, and my belly button is an inch lower than it used to be. It took me a while, but I figured it out. When I saw the canisters and how at ease the Rrassic were with them, it told me that there was a bit more to our existence than I thought."

Niiva sighed. "You don't mind?"

"I was never one for a theology that said your soul was linked to someone's vagina. I am me, no matter where I came from."

They continued discussing their situation for a few minutes, and then, Bree got the law books out again and started quizzing. Bree was leaving in two or three days, so it was best to get as much assistance from her as possible.

The secure vehicle rushed through the darkness, and the different checkpoints caught their excitement.

Argo was nearly crushing Niiva's hand in his nervous enthusiasm, and she couldn't blame him. They were about to watch the first human-Rrassic decanting. Bree's baby was the start of a whole new generation of hope.

When they checked in at the front desk, the tension in the entire building was palpable.

"This is going to be us in a few months." Argo murmured it to her as they walked under escort to the decanting area.

"It is going to be bizarre. We have already contributed six out of our twenty. I almost wish that it wasn't happening so fast."

"It will just make time for our time together as peacekeepers. You will want to have a firm presence by the time our daughters return to us."

She smiled. "There is one son in the mix."

"He will grow up to know that he is part of an important family, and hopefully, he will inherit my sex drive and not yours. No offense, pet."

She laughed. "You only call me pet when you mean offense. It is fine. I don't want my son to screw his way through the population either."

Argo chuckled. "He will be taught self-control, as we all were."

They entered the decanting area where a small medical station had been set up in the centre of the space. Floating vid cameras were around the area, and the mated humans and their chosen Rrassic were standing a respectful distance back from the expectant family.

Bree saw her and gave a teary grin and a thumbs-up. Arix had his arm around her as they watched the canister being removed from its place in the library and carried carefully to the central station.

The baby nearly filled the canister, and the unit was glowing with a soft blue light.

Iktabi smiled and spoke. "Thank you, Bree and Arix, for this contribution to the future of the Rrassic. Your names will be inscribed in our history."

Bree sighed. "Great. I want to hold my baby."

Iktabi backed away, and in the shadows, Niiva watched Lekorh standing with his hood drawn and a smaller figure next to him. Sarah seemed to be going through some kind of Saya training.

Sarah pulled her hood back slightly and winked at Niiva, indicating that she was listening to all thoughts in the room.

Lekorh's head turned toward Sarah, and she reset her hood and kept it blankly forward.

The canister was opened, and the little girl was eased into the world, wet and slippery, but Bree was holding her as soon as she was wrapped.

Arix held both his mate and child in his arms; his colouration was rippling with colours Niiva had never seen on a Luthin.

Argo pulled her against him, and she smiled. No one was speaking. This moment was important to them all.

The little silvery girl coughed softly, and then, she let out a wail that had all the women in the room laughing. Arix beamed, Iktabi looked alarmed, and Sorrok was smiling ruefully. A glance up at Argo showed his fascination with the little fingers and toes exposed by the loose wrapping.

Niiva sighed. "When we have our collection, we can head

to the creche and raise our brood if you like. As long as I have help with all the little ones, we can do it."

He smiled. "Are you sure?"

"I am sure. We can take them and raise them until they are old enough to enter into Rrassic training. Is it a deal?"

He squeezed her. "Deal."

Twenty children at the same time in a dimensional bubble where time moved faster was the stuff of science fiction but so was being a human-alien hybrid. Niiva had some time to learn about what raising that many children would entail, and she knew that it was going to be more involved than rearing goats.

She would take on that challenge when they had their twenty, and with the way her body was producing eggs, it would be sooner than she would like.

Her career would have to be put on hold when the time came, like many women before her, she would have to put her plans on hold for family. When she watched Argo looking over at the baby, she decided that she didn't really mind.

She would make him pay for her generosity later and at random intervals. He always rose to her challenge, and it was what she loved most about him. Well, that and his abs, but it was far less poetic to focus on the physical, even if it was true.

"Come on, you big kitty. Let's see if we can hold the baby."

She pulled him forward, and when Bree handed over the little warm bundle, Niiva knew she saw her own future, and it wasn't as overwhelming as she thought it would be. Argo would be an attentive caregiver, and she could handle the heavy lifting. Yeah, a future with children was possible, even if it hadn't precisely been in her plans, but then, her plans had gone out the window when she had been snatched, cloned, and offered as a mate to the alien hordes. Things couldn't have turned out better.

The human-Rrassic hybrid in her arms was named while she held it. Bree stroked the soft cheek and murmured, "Remi. Remi Bree-Arix. First human-Rrassic on Imrahl."

Niiva handed the baby back to her mother. "Remi is a very good name."

Back with Argo, she glanced over at the library wall where their canisters were lining up. "Oh, shit. We have to name them all."

His shoulders shook, and he wrapped her in his arms. "We have time, Niiva. We have time."

Author's Note

Finally! After a rough 2018, I was able to start 2019 with Brace for Humanity. It has been designed as a six-part series, and now, we are in the final arc. Whew.

My intent is to finish this series back to back, so hopefully, it will come out in a fairly tight grouping.

The next book is Sarah's. She is the companion in *Companion's Dilemma*. Going from highly intuitive to telepathy isn't a journey without pain, and she earns every milestone she gets before someone notices that her skills have become exceptional.

Thanks for reading,

Viola Grace

ABOUT THE AUTHOR

Viola Grace (aka Zenina Masters) is a Canadian sci-fi/ paranormal romance writer with ambitions to keep writing for the rest of her life. She specializes in short stories because the thrill of discovery, of all those firsts, is what keeps her writing.

An artist who enjoys a story that catches you up, whirls you around, and sets you down with a smile on your face is all she endeavours to be. She prefers to leave the drama to those who are better suited to it, she always goes for the cheap laugh.

In real life, she now is engaged in beekeeping, and her adventures can be found on the YouTube channel, Mystery Bees Apiary. Just look for the cartoon kittens.